CUTHBERT
Tea for Two in the Valley

#3

by

Patrick Barrett

A Wild Wolf Publication

Published by Wild Wolf Publishing in 2016
Copyright © 2016 Patrick Barrett

ISBN: 978-1-907954-52-8
Also available as an e-book

www.wildwolfpublishing.com

I am once again dedicating the third book in the Cuthbert series to my beautiful wife, Paula Jayne, without whom these books would never have seen the light of day.

Chapter One

The crow stretched luxuriously, the sun warming his back as he sent a ripple of waking pleasure through his feathers. A distant shout, followed by a 'clop' sound, caused him to open one eye. 'Surely it's not the cricket season again,' he thought.

Crows the world over gained immense pleasure from watching the antics of the 'Men in white'. It was always hard to tell from above whether it was cricket or Morris Dancing.

A sound and a change in approaching air pressure began to concern the crow, and he opened the other eye in time to see a white missile blur past, before the slip-stream spun him out of the tree in a downward spiral of curses and feathers.

Some distance away, a group of strangely clad men gathered and shielded their eyes from the sun as they discussed trajectory and style.

"Any higher and it would have been a moon-shot," sniggered Ronald Chisolm.

Percy glared from beneath his new tartan cap and clunked away from the group, slapping away at a piece of wood stuck onto his new spiked shoe.

He had trodden on the plank some time ago and had tried to dislodge it at every subtle opportunity without admitting that it was there. He had even ignored Cuthbert's solicitous, "Are you limping, Percy?"

The others watched him clunk away and Henry Chisolm placed the small white ball onto its plastic tee. Somehow, Henry did not look ridiculous in his playing gear. Cuthbert decided that it was a matter of mind over fashion; pretend it belonged and the body would not betray its embarrassment.

Henry positioned himself over the ball and waggled his hips, gazing into the distance. With an effortless swing and a cry of "Fore!" he propelled the ball into a climbing curve heading straight for the taunting little flag in the distance.

Cuthbert tried to organise his limbs in the same manner as he strode up to the tee. Hip-wobbling didn't come naturally to him and he used the moment to ease his aching back.

It seemed particularly pointless carrying a heavy bag full of clubs when he was missing quite adequately with the same one every time. Cuthbert lined up his shot. The club felt at home in his hands and his muscles vibrated eagerly.

He swung.

Peering into the distance, Cuthbert could not contain his glee. The ball was out of sight, the connection had been smooth and the swing faultless. Trying desperately not to be smug, Cuthbert took a step forward to clear the tee.

"Don't tread on the ball, Cuthbert," said Henry as he walked away.

There it lay! If a ball could wink, it would have done. Cuthbert stared at it in disbelief. Ronald laid a sympathetic hand on Cuthbert's shoulder and commiserated.

"It's no big deal, Cuthbert." He patted him gently. "I could see the problem, but it would have put you off your stroke if I had said anything."

Cuthbert brightened slightly. "Oh right, so what is the problem, then?"

Ronald looked into Cuthbert's eager face and confided, "You are standing too close to the ball ... after you've hit it!" With a last slap on Cuthbert's shoulder, Ronald went after his brother, roaring with laughter.

Cuthbert slumped under the weight of his woes and then slumped again under the weight of his bag as he trailed after the others. Nothing could lift him from his gloom as he trudged wearily along.

Then he spotted Percy - at least he thought it was Percy. A tartan cap was haring about all over the place like a broken clockwork toy, but it was only a couple of inches above the ground. As usual, Cuthbert relied upon Percy to distract him from everything else. It was a kind of therapy simply knowing Percy.

A shout from the tree-line caused Cuthbert to head in that direction. Percy seemed to be hanging upside down from a large branch with clubs scattered around beneath him, his mop of unruly red hair glowing in the sun.

"Is there any point in me asking what happened?" asked Cuthbert.

Percy spluttered somewhere between rage and asphyxia, "Bird ... pecking ball to death ... climbed above it ... hat fell off ... get me down."

The spikes in Percy's shoes were firmly embedded into the branch and the knots in his laces would have made a sailor wince. Cuthbert climbed up onto the branch and simply cut the laces, feeling the branch spring back to its normal place and hearing a yelp from below.

By the time Cuthbert had climbed down, Percy was racing around in circles swinging a club at a tartan hat which had now sprouted wings and perfected huge gliding leaps.

Cuthbert collected all the discarded clubs and was actually whistling as he set off home.

Chapter Two

The bar of the Mandrake Arms looked just as it did on any other night of the week, but tonight there were subtle differences.

The laughter was louder and consisted of hearty guffaws, the conversation was sprinkled with coded references to 'birdies' and 'eagles', and people insisted upon suddenly swinging their arms towards the roof beams to demonstrate some unique shot or other.

"Why is he laughing like that?" asked Percy, nodding towards Henry.

Cuthbert looked across and answered him with, "Why are we dressed like this?"

Percy considered this and asked, "Will every night be like this now?"

Cuthbert leaned back in his chair and replied, "No, from now on after every game, the pub becomes the 'Club House' and we all sit here in these ridiculous outfits blathering on about who hit what, where and why."

Percy suddenly grinned as he contributed, "Or, in your case, who didn't hit anything, anywhere for anyone."

Cuthbert was offended. "It's hardly natural, is it, hitting a ball around the countryside and hoping it rolls into a hole obviously too small to catch it."

Percy hid his grin behind a dimpled pint glass which had the effect of making his eyes glide apart alarmingly.

Cuthbert looked away.

Chapter Three

The Valley had settled down nicely after all the chaos caused by Aunt Liza and her cinema complex.

Cuthbert had moved the theatre productions into the shell of the huge cinema building because the old barn creaked so badly that the cast could barely be heard.

Not that the audience noticed, but apparently one could fail to achieve a safety certificate if one yelled 'Fire!' and nobody heard.

The sudden passion for golf had begun with Henry and Ronald Chisolm. Apparently, before the old Hall burnt down, they had planned to build a private golf course behind it, but with Percy's shed having squatter's rights and the balls disappearing into the old tunnel systems, it all seemed too much effort.

Now, however, everyone seemed to have more leisure time and the hunt was on for a 'gentlemanly pursuit' to unite the Valley folk.

To Cuthbert and Percy, it seemed like the ultimate humiliation. How on earth could anyone take it all seriously? Why did anyone care whether one person had more balls in holes than another? Cuthbert had left all that behind when he gave up marbles.

Then there was the clothing. Good grief! Talk about a clever tailor with abandoned stock, using colour blind designers to make a profit. This man had invented a money machine. No rivals had ever appeared, because no-one believed it had happened in the first place.

Then there was the equipment: titanium shafts with ebony laminated heads, handles made from nitro-ferrous pancake mix, and because they couldn't seem to get the shape right, you had to carry twelve of the damned things! So, of course, the brains behind it all came up with a special bag made from discarded RAF windsocks. Wherever the genius behind this lot was now, he certainly wouldn't be out playing golf.

Cuthbert's reverie was interrupted by a threatening rumble which stopped the conversation dead.

The only person in the Valley who could achieve this effect was now glowering at Henry and Ronald with a look which could transform a riot into a Madame Tussaud's tableau in seconds.

Henry's daughter did have a name, but no-one seemed to know what it was. The Valley generally knew her as Arkle due to her remarkable resemblance to the famous racehorse. At this moment she was drawing herself into a mountain of tweed and indignation as she hissed, "What did you say?"

Ronald paused with his glass in mid-air, then thinking tactically, he set it down on the bar, out of her reach. This was the man who, according to his own legends, had cleared all the corners of the globe of the description 'Here be monsters'. He had toppled giants and trampled pygmies and all eyes were upon him.

"Well," he stammered, "it's genetic, isn't it? A woman can't concentrate long enough to make a ball go where it's needed enough times to ever win a game of golf."

Henry tried to step in to ease his brother's plight, but his wife Margery paused from cleaning a glass and gave him a warning look. Henry wisely took a drink.

Arkle moved slowly as she stepped up close to Ronald and rumbled, "Would you redundant hunter-gatherers care to challenge the weaker sex?"

Now, Ronald suddenly had trouble equating Arkle with the weaker sex in any way, shape or form, but his hesitation was taken as cowardice.

"Thought not," trumpeted Arkle. "Typical man, always planning the battles, but never there to do the washing-up afterwards."

Again Ronald was completely wrong-footed by images of why there should have been a pile of washing-up after Waterloo. His hesitation seemed to reinforce Arkle's stance.

Realising that he needed to make up some ground quickly, he blurted out, "You name the prize, then," and in a moment of desperation he went too far, "... and you can even pick the teams." Ronald stood smugly content until he realised that everyone else was holding their collective breath.

Arkle turned slowly and fixed a certain table with a triumphant look. "Done," she whispered as Cuthbert and Percy withered under her stare.

Gales of female laughter followed them down the street. Cuthbert and Percy had slunk out of the bar as all eyes had swivelled towards them.

The women scented victory immediately and the men were stricken with foreboding. As they trudged home through the dusk, Percy peered out from under his cap and asked, "How did we walk into that one?"

Cuthbert sighed. "We don't even have to walk into anything these days, it happens when we're sitting down. I told you that kicking a crow was bad luck."

Percy grinned. "It certainly was for the crow."

Chapter Four

The next morning, Percy was back to thumping into the village in his folded-down wellies.

Neither he nor Cuthbert could remember which tree his golf shoes had attached themselves to. The new tartan hat was still a novelty, though, and he wore it proudly.

Approaching the village green, he spotted a line-up of local women all reaching and stretching in unison under the command of Arkle who stood facing them.

Percy sidled up to Avril, the local journalist from the 'Triple Echo'. "What's happening?"

Avril replied, "Tai-chi."

Percy looked puzzled. "I thought that was a Panda."

Avril realised who she was talking to and made it simple. "Cardio-vascular exercise of varying speeds and intensities to encourage aerobic performance."

Percy was impressed. "Not a Panda, then?"

Avril closed her notebook with a snap and walked away.

Percy watched for a moment until the women began practising golf strokes and it all came back to him. "Oh-oh," he muttered and headed for the pub.

The bar was silent; full, but silent. Ronald sat alone at one end of the bar and the rest of the men folk were huddled as far away as possible, peering into their drinks as if hunting for the King's shilling. Percy accepted a pint from a subdued Henry and joined the huddle of melancholia in the corner.

Percy took a long drink and asked, "Who is in the team, then?"

Captain Edgar answered morosely, "You two, mostly." There didn't seem any need to say anything else.

Percy tried to lighten the mood a little. "So what's the worst that can happen, eh?"

Several voices answered at once. "We change places with the women for six months."

Percy cheered visibly. "Oh yes, good one, that's the spirit, lads."

The faces around him stayed as stone. No-one spoke. Percy gulped, muttered, "I'll have a word with Cuthbert," and ran.

Chapter Five

Cuthbert was trying desperately to imagine what it would all mean. "But we can't. They do all the ... and they are always doing ... what if they didn't ...? Oh, good grief."

After a few moments of silent contemplation over the kitchen table, the knock at the door came as a shock. A committee stood on the doorstep.

Henry and Ronald, Captain Edgar, even Constable Beeching and Jasper, the Head of the Village Mafia, standing close together without handcuffs. This was serious.

They all collected in the farmyard, sitting on various upturned barrels, boxes and old bits of farm stuff which no-one recognised.

Henry announced, "We need a team of five. The women have picked the first two for us." With a sigh, he nodded to the two reluctant heroes, Cuthbert and Percy.

"I will play, and of course, Ronald owes us the game of his life." Henry paused and surveyed the throng. "Constable Beeching accepts that he cannot actually reach around his own stomach to grip his club and the thought of walking gives him a panic attack. We really need Jasper for our 'dirty-tricks' department and the clubs are longer than he is anyway. So, gentlemen, we need a fifth man. Any suggestions?"

"What about the Captain?" Cuthbert asked.

Captain Edgar shuffled uncomfortably. "Loads of problems with the little woman. If I play, she will play and she is excellent. I am trying to narrow the odds a little."

Percy came in several sentences later and asked, "What dirty tricks department?"

Henry replied, "Let's not mince words, gentlemen. The last time I saw Arkle hit a ball, the skin peeled from it like a banana when it took off."

Several people blanched but Jasper asked, "How many points did that score?"

Henry replied irritably, "None, of course."

Jasper smiled. "Exactly, we have to exploit their weaknesses, that way they will be ours." He couldn't resist a glance at Cuthbert. "And with a little tampering, we could well take the initiative."

The others relaxed; this was more like it, this was a competition for real men. Cheating had an honest ring about it.

The afternoon was scheduled as a tutorial. The Captain would assist with the teaching and help out in general.

Chapter Six

The Captain and Henry were practising strokes when Percy and Cuthbert appeared. Henry gasped.

Percy was waddling towards them with a club handle stuck down each welly. He looked like a short John Wayne with two long-barrelled guns.

Cuthbert was dragging a huge farm sack full of clubs and croquet mallets behind him, leaving a furrow in the ground.

"One extreme to the other," muttered Henry. "What are you doing, Cuthbert?" he asked.

Cuthbert paused and laid down the sack. "I sorted through the attic. There's everything in there, nibblers, nobblers, wedges, woods and a thing like a corkscrew for clearing drains."

Henry turned to Percy. "And your excuse?"

Percy tapped the side of his nose. "Why carry all that lot? I've got a big one and a little one." He grinned as if the prize had already been won.

Henry sighed. He had drilled two holes in the floor and set up a pitch and putt course. "Right, let's have a knock about and find your strengths."

Ronald laughed darkly, but as this was completely his fault, he kept his thoughts to himself.

Henry bent down to move a barrel out of the way just as a ball sailed over his head and landed smack in the hole. "Who did that?" he asked.

Cuthbert replied, "Me."

Henry looked at him in amazement. "I thought you couldn't play …"

Cuthbert explained, "I am an undertaker, you know. We used to play crazy golf with the corpses when I was an apprentice. There aren't many places I can't hit in this farmyard."

Henry looked at him sceptically and then started re-arranging things as obstacles. "All right, Cuthbert, off you go."

Cuthbert chose an old cane-handled club, which really should have been on a museum wall, and squinted along the ground. "Stand back," he called.

"He means 'fore'," supplied Percy.

Cuthbert swung the club and the ball set off wobbling along an old tyre rut. Avoiding the barrel, it rolled past the hole to a snort of derision from Ronald, before rolling sideways along a piece of corrugated iron sheeting and rolling back into the hole.

It took all afternoon to convince them that he could indeed hole the ball regardless of any obstacle laid in the farmyard.

He even lobbed one ball onto the barn roof, where it rolled into the guttering, down the drainpipe into the trough, out of the broken corner and into the hole.

Unfortunately, he was absolutely hopeless at simply driving the thing in a straight line in open countryside.

Percy was put through his paces next and appeared to have a fairly powerful drive. Direction, though, was a real problem.

Every time he struck the ball, it left the club at a sixty degree angle. Several attempts to get him to aim-off seemed to show promise. If they pointed him sixty degrees away from the hole, he started to get close, but it was unnerving standing anywhere near him.

After all this practice, the weary team gathered around Cuthbert's table. They still needed a fifth man and they were discussing this when Jasper appeared. "I have been in touch with the twins," he announced. "They have given me permission to use their notes and will try to be here on the day. There is some talk of radio-controlled devices and laser direction finders, so we have that for a back-up."

The team acknowledged his efforts warily. "We can also link up with personal radios to keep in touch and pass on advice if we can disguise them."

Percy looked up. "You could hide one in my hat."

Jasper looked concerned. "No, better not, we may need it again."

Percy looked insulted for a moment and then asked, "Did I ever tell you about …?" He shuffled to get comfortable and looked around. He was alone. 'Oh,' he thought and shambled off to bed.

Chapter Seven

The next morning brought another deputation to Cuthbert's door. This time it was the women, and they were smiling.

Women very rarely smiled at Cuthbert, either in his role as the local undertaker (when they tended to be grieving), or in his role as Cuthbert (when they tended to be wary).

All three of these women were smiling at him and they had brought him home baking!

The internal alarm bells were starting to clonk heavily as Cuthbert let his visitors in. The last woman who offered him home baking needed a death certificate which had absolutely no acquaintance with the truth and the ink was still wet on the insurance policy.

The ladies sat down around Cuthbert's kitchen table, or two of them did. Margery, Henry's wife, placed the basket firmly in the centre of the table and sat down demurely. Arkle seemed to kick a space in the row of chairs, sending the others screeching and skittering away across the flagstones in panic.

Avril, the reporter from the 'Triple Echo' newspaper stood back against the wall staring in horror at the long scrubbed pine table stretching before her. "Is this where ...?" she stammered.

"No, dear," replied Margery. "He has a place out the back."

Avril then looked around at a huge pan bubbling on an evil-looking cooking range. "Is that ...?"

Margery sighed. "No, dear, they're probably his socks."

Cuthbert, ever the attentive host, didn't have the faintest idea what was going on and was beginning to suspect that they just wanted to borrow his kitchen for a meeting of some sort.

Carefully avoiding Avril, who shrank away as if Dracula had just licked her neck, Cuthbert tried to sidle away quietly.

His last encounter with Avril had not been a happy one. He had been fascinated by the wire spiral on her notebook and she had thought that he was staring down her blouse. Now, whenever they met, Avril was always zipped up to the neck and held her notebook as if to ward off evil spirits.

Cuthbert was halfway to the door when a chair opposite Arkle shot out backwards and stopped him.

"Take a seat!" boomed Arkle in the 'whipper-in' voice she used to terrify whole packs of hounds.

Cuthbert tucked in his 'tail' and sat.

Margery waited for Avril who seemed to hover above her chair with huge eyes like Bambi ready for flight. With a flourish, Margery removed the cover from the basket and produced three plates of offerings.

The first was a plate of perfectly formed pastries from Margery's own fair hand, with scalloped edges and a dainty little cross cut in each one, the second had obviously just been bought from Mrs. Biggle at the Post Office and unwrapped hastily, and the third pile resembled pastry doughnuts except that the hole was where Arkle had jammed her thumb into the middle to make the lids stay on.

Cuthbert muttered his appreciation as two sets of femininity focused on him. Cuthbert could not bring himself to look at Arkle; it was too much to contemplate.

"Now," Margery purred, "we were wondering about the play, Cuthbert."

Cuthbert was taken by surprise. However, since this was his natural state, he showed no sign of it and simply replied, "Ahh, the play," while watching a lead scout from the ant colony under the range waggle its antennae over the edge of the table. He nodded wisely, playing for time and watching the exits.

Margery continued, "It must be time to start rehearsals and we don't even know which play you are putting on."

Cuthbert glanced at Avril and she waved her notebook weakly as if that explained everything.

"Tradition!" boomed Arkle. She thumped the table, causing the cakes to leap up and re-arrange themselves, and the forcing the ant to demonstrate high altitude, low opening techniques to his mates waiting below.

Cuthbert looked from face to face. "But we haven't moved into the new building yet," he spluttered.

Cries of, "Simple," "Not a problem," and a wave of the notebook greeted this statement. The chatter flew back and forth past Cuthbert like Wimbledon volleys and suddenly Cuthbert was alone with a terrible feeling that he had just agreed to stage a production of 'Taming of the Shrew' in just a few weeks' time.

Percy crashed into the kitchen expecting all the chairs to be where they were supposed to be and spotted the cakes.

"Oh well done, Cuthbert. You have been busy," he said, grabbing a cake covered in ants and stuffing it in his mouth. "The currants are a nice touch."

Cuthbert sat staring into space. He had just been manipulated. He should know; he was a martyr to it. His headstone would probably read 'I was manipulated into this,' or 'This was not a burial; it was a manipulation'. He was only stopped from plunging into the depths of depression by seeing Percy with crumbs on his chin and ants up his nose.

Chapter Eight

Meeting the rest of the golf team later that day, Cuthbert explained the early morning visit from the opposition.

They met in the park, away from prying ears. Percy even checked the litter bin thoroughly. *What is it with Percy and that litter bin?* As a team, they were soon onto the women's ploy.

Ronald contributed, "We won't have time to practise."

Henry could see problems with the lead character being bullied by his wife over several weeks on stage. "Lots of chances for accidents there," he mused, "and the men all carry swords."

Behind them, Percy's wellies waved in the air as he checked for eavesdroppers and promptly fell into the litter-bin.

Back in Cuthbert's kitchen, the men discussed tactics while toying with the cakes.

Percy was quite down. "I never wanted to play golf anyway. What's the point of walking all that way to end up back where you started, having to buy more balls before you can set off again?" he moaned.

No-one argued. The men didn't really have busy lives, but it was important to maintain the façade of busy lives. Now this was in jeopardy.

Percy was still mumbling to himself when he suddenly brightened. "You know, it's not the end of the world if you're not good at something. My family has a history of printing and not one of them could read or write."

Time seemed to stop around the table. No-one ever admitted to it afterwards, but someone said, "How did that work, then, Percy?"

Percy shuffled to get comfortable and began. "Well, many years ago, one of my ancestors was a cleaner and odd-job man for a chap who invented the first printing machine.

The printer used to stamp adverts on the backs of my ancestor's hands and send him out waving to people. The locals thought he had a delusion about being royal and simply waved back.

Anyway, the inventor chap died during the night just as the Prince of the Realm, the local Mayor and his full Council were about to visit the next day.

Obviously my ancestor was going to be out of a job, so he tried on some of his late boss's clothes, just for his next interview, you understand.

Anyway, he was still wearing his boss's smart clothes when the Prince arrived with his retinue. Right bunch of snobs they were; they never looked directly at a peasant or tradesman, so they didn't notice anything amiss. My ancestor got sucked into the situation and started to demonstrate the printing machine.

He chucked a load of letters into the trays and wound the handle down, then showed the sheet of paper to his visitors. Now, none of this bunch could read either, but no-one was going to admit it in front of the others or to a common tradesman, so they all ordered copies and started libraries in their homes.

My ancestor simply stayed in the deceased printer's house and kept them all supplied as they built more shelves and needed more books to fill them; it lasted for generations, that game did."

Percy sat back, bathing in the attention, and Henry asked, "No-one ever twigged in all that time?"

Percy leaned forward again. "The thing was, the church muttered away in Latin, the money lenders spoke in code and the villains had a rhyming slang. So, whichever language a chap used, my ancestor told him it was written in the other language. By the time anyone was educated enough, another generation had passed and the man in charge could say, 'Ahh,that was my father you spoke to, sir. Is there anything I can do for you?'"

Ronald fixed Percy with a sceptical eye and asked, "So why aren't you printing, then?"

Percy deflated somewhat. "It was education that did it for us in the end. Who would have thought that anyone would bother teaching children to read? Suddenly, there was a generation of nosy kids wanting to know what their parents' estates were worth and they were trying to find rare works in the libraries. We bluffed for a while, claiming that they were books of secret magic spells in Aramaic, but some foreigner opened a kebab stall nearby and said he couldn't read them either."

"What happened?" asked Cuthbert for the sake of joining in.

20

"Oh," Percy sighed, "a neighbour, Mr. Mills, borrowed some money and joined up with someone named Boon, and they bought us out."

The assembly nodded wisely and all gradually made their way home.

Chapter Nine

The crow watched very carefully as Cuthbert and Percy practised outside.

There was hardly a single calamity which hadn't befallen this bird and these two had never been far away.

He would move away but there were certain fallacies about crows. 'As the crow flies' wasn't about economy of movement at all; they just had lousy memories and if they didn't get back quickly they were lost. And by reasoning that when you are lost, you are no longer at home, they simply stayed where they were.

Percy was trying out his new strategy. He had painted arrows on his wellies so that he knew which way to face when he 'aimed-off.' This had been difficult and he had fallen off the sundial twice already.

As if that wasn't bad enough, in his hurry to try out the new method, he had put them on the wrong feet and it was all taking some sorting out.

Cuthbert was trying to keep a wall between them every time Percy swung his club. As for Cuthbert, he simply could not drive a ball in a straight line.

Henry had taken them to a driving range for intense practice. They were installed on the upper tier and Cuthbert couldn't understand why the chap below shouted 'Thank you' every time he sliced and the ball rolled over the edge.

Percy had been machine-gunned by the automatic ball firer and Henry was harangued for bringing 'Care in the community' patients out on a weekend. The exercise had not been a success at all.

Now, at least they had the peace to simply slog away at the problem without strange advice in arcane language separated by unfathomable jargon. 'Bogey' for instance had to be avoided around Percy at all costs.

Chapter Ten

Cuthbert had spent the morning at the empty shell of the cinema. Some of the furniture and props had been moved in and they were dwarfed by the vast building.

Cuthbert was beginning to picture either a gigantic stage where the actors would need loud-hailers or thousands of seats with nobody to keep them all warm.

The old building had been used for plays for generations and had atmosphere; it had seen every type of mistake, accident or tragedy. They would have a clean slate in this building. Cuthbert wondered if they would have to break it in, like a new wok.

A performance of 'Taming of the Shrew' starring the two rival factions should do the trick, he thought. Percy and Cuthbert had stayed up late into the night discussing the plays and wondered about customising them to fit the community.

They came up with 'The Gardener of Venice,' starring Percy - mostly involving water features, Homicidal Ronald in 'Macbeth', Henry and Margery in 'Romeo and Juliet', with 'Much ado about Nothing' to reflect Cuthbert's impact on the Valley.

Of course, the real Valley folk would not allow tampering with the Bard. Legend had it that Shakespeare himself had worked as a teacher in the Valley and written several plays here, hence the obsession with keeping his performances alive via the annual play.

Cuthbert looked around the cavernous interior of the building and old dreams of staging real chariot races came flooding back.

His resident hero had always been the local milkman. He drove his horse-drawn cart as if auditioning for the Circus Maximus and he had pearly white teeth; what more could a producer ask?

Cuthbert sighed. The cart was stored in one of Cuthbert's out-buildings and the horse had been put out to grass. The milkman had gone 'travelling.'

The modern world had become too much for him: motorised deliveries and milk so full of chemicals it refused point-blank to go off in warm weather.

The final straw had been the carton - milk in a cardboard conundrum. Who in their right mind wanted to wrestle with one of those things first thing in the morning?

The milkman firmly believed that this was the reason for malnourished school children. They could not open the thing in time to eat breakfast.

Anyway, the milkman had gone to 'find himself'. Percy maintained that he had gone to find the inventor of the carton and strangle him.

Cuthbert thought back briefly over the adventures they had all shared in the past. Just when things had settled down, Ronald ignited something else. Perhaps that's why the Valley was unique.

Chapter Eleven

Percy was having trouble. He suspected that this new tartan cap didn't work as well as his scruffy old one.

Jasper had been showing him some plans for devices and Percy just couldn't get to grips with it.

He'd tried all the usual tricks - scratching his head to play for time and nodding wisely while someone else solved it - and he was now reduced to walking around with a tape measure pulled partly out as if searching for materials. Between Jasper and the plans the twins had sent, there was a definite headache coming on.

"Come on, Percy, I saw the coconut launcher you made out of a tractor," said Jasper. "Surely you can handle this?" He stood surrounded by blue-prints and diagrams from the twins' war chest, wondering what the problem was.

Percy stopped and turned. "Look," he said, jumping a foot as the tape measure retracted suddenly. "I don't get on with electrics. The reason I stay in the Valley is because we don't have electrics, and when we do it doesn't last very long."

He paused to collect his thoughts and fears, and confided, "Electric is sneaky. You can't see it, you can't hear it and when it grabs you, it won't let go." He looked kindly at the eager young man. "Look, son, not everything new in life is an improvement. Name one way that electrics have improved my life."

Jasper barely hesitated. "Lights, cooking and heating," he tried.

Percy fired back, "Hurts my eyes, dries out my food and makes my wellies smell."

Jasper narrowed his eyes and tried, "Television, radio and computers."

Percy retorted, "Hurts my eyes, hurts my ears and hurts my brain.

Jasper tried again. "Kettles, toasters and microwaves."

Percy looked at him pityingly. "Box of matches and some sticks."

Jasper gave up, rolled up the plans and went in search of someone more advanced than Percy. Any school-kid should fit the bill.

Percy was content. His superior reasoning powers had won again. Still, he liked the look of the plan where you drilled holes in the balls and …

Chapter Twelve

Cuthbert meanwhile had waited for the library van. It usually bumbled into the village once a month and Mrs. Page would offer all kinds of literary wonders to the population.

Waiting politely until the engine gave one last cough and the door swung back like a shutter in a tornado, Cuthbert climbed aboard.

"Morning, Mrs. Page," chanted Cuthbert as if he were still in infant school.

Mrs. Page peered over her half-moon glasses and said "Good morrow, young sir. Went the day well?"

Cuthbert had forgotten that Mrs. Page always spoke in the manner of the current book she was reading.

"Tis well met this fine morning, is it not? Please don't tarry, young sir. I am due at yonder castle."

"Yes, it is not well this morrow morning yet," tried Cuthbert, gamely guessing that she was reading historical fiction this week, before starting to search for books on golf tuition.

The shelf had a very obvious space between 'Fencing' and 'Hop-scotch.' Cuthbert looked down the length of the van and thought Mrs. Page was sitting slightly higher than usual.

"Anything on golf, by any chance?" asked Cuthbert.

Mrs. Page hesitated. The shifty look suggested that her current reading matter obviously didn't involve hitting things with sticks.

"I would really like to see a book on golf, please," said Cuthbert, moving down the van, convinced that Mrs. Page was not at a comfortable driving height.

Mrs Page pushed the half hidden book further beneath her and hissed, "Be careful what you wish for, young man. It may not be the lesson you were seeking," as she reverted to last week's oriental philosophy.

Cuthbert tried, "If you show me the book, I can soon decide."

"Ah, decisions," said Mrs. Page wistfully as she stamped on the accelerator.

The old van reared and leapt forward. Cuthbert, though desperately trying to keep his place amid time and motion, slid backwards until he was ejected from the back of the van and dumped in the road amidst a flock of sheep.

The sheep milled uselessly about him and Blind Pugh, the sheepdog, cocked his head to one side, listening for a clue as to where to bite.

Cuthbert brushed himself down as he stood glaring at the dust cloud which screamed to a halt outside the Mandrake Arms and a hand was seen passing a book to Margery before the cloud moved on again o'er dale and hill.

Blind Pugh had obviously mistaken the escaping van for the local bus and herded the sheep into the road. Cuthbert pushed through the flock, looked at Blind Pugh, and snapped, "You're getting old," in an attempt to make someone feel worse than him.

Blind Pugh lunged and missed.

"So," muttered Cuthbert, "the conspiracies begin and it's every man for himself, eh?"

The walk back to Cuthbert's home seemed to take on a strange quality. He no longer saw the landscape as something to be trodden on.

It now became a series of obstacles with cunningly placed obstructions. He found himself planning which club to use if the flag was just over the fence or on the other side of that stream.

What if the flag was beyond those trees and in the fold of those hills? Would he land the ball on the slope and let it roll down gently or power it straight over the trees?

Cuthbert mentally cleared the image. This was becoming weird. A time-consuming knock-about was one thing but obsessing about terrain was quite another.

He walked on through the once again familiar landscape. The sun shone and the bees hummed by, one after the other and very loudly.

Cuthbert ducked and hid behind a large galvanised milk-churn. The churn resonated like an old funeral bell as a golf ball ricocheted off it.

The things were coming thick and fast now as if some maniac had invented a machine gun for firing golf balls.

"Percy!" yelled Cuthbert as he zigzagged across a field. Ahead of him a cow chewed quietly, its dark eyes swinging from side to side as a golf ball whizzed by, first one side and then the other.

As Cuthbert passed the creature, its brain decided that chewing and watching simultaneously were beyond the call of duty and it fell over exhausted.

Cuthbert reached the outbuildings and used natural cover to close up on the suspected source of the fusillade.

"About time, Cuthbert," shouted Percy. "Anymore golf balls in that attic of yours?"

Cuthbert approached warily. Percy was glowing, always a bad sign.

"What do you think, then?"

Percy was wiping his hands on an oily rag which mysteriously always appeared when he was pleased with one of his creations. Cuthbert looked.

His old tractor was still up on blocks with the back wheels taken off as it had been since being used as an assault weapon in the great cinema wars.

Percy had replaced the pipes with a smaller bore version and fitted a hopper. Cuthbert recognised the hopper as being from the muck-spreader.

'No wonder the balls hummed,' he thought to himself.

Percy had turned off the engine when he ran out of balls and stood beaming at Cuthbert like a retriever presenting its owner with a stunned duck.

Cuthbert walked around the contraption. He stroked his chin and even kicked the tyres. He knew Percy well enough by now and certain formalities had to be followed to avoid the sulks. "Where precisely does this fit into the scheme of things?" he asked.

Percy sighed. Sometimes he wondered about Cuthbert. He didn't seem very quick on the uptake some days. "The hopper holds four thousand balls. If we fire four thousand balls in succession, it will saturate the green and some are bound to roll into the hole. It saves all that walking, see?" He paused and continued to beam.

Cuthbert needed to tread gently. "Four thousand balls, eh?" he mused. "Does it say that in the handbook?"

Percy shook his head as if reasoning with a foreigner. "Cuthbert, if you chuck a ball into the hopper it makes a 'clunk'. When it rolls out again, you chuck it back in, if you count the clunks, that gives you the total amount of balls it will hold. Simple engineering mathematics, that is."

Cuthbert watched Percy wiping his hands and sucked desperately on his bottom lip until he could ask. "So, it was the same ball every time, then, Percy?"

Percy narrowed his eyes suspiciously. "Of course it was. It's not my fault that you were three thousand and eight hundred balls short of a load."

Cuthbert pushed the point with, "So, how did you know when the hopper was full, then?"

Percy squirmed slightly, "Well, it's not an exact science. After chucking a ball in for three hours it gets tiring, so it's a matter of calculating the ratio of clunks to remaining space. That's empirical, that is." Percy beamed proudly.

Cuthbert's bottom lip was starting to hurt, so he asked, "Aren't there rules about that sort of thing in competitions?" He then asked, "What if the women turn up with a machine holding five thousand balls and the whole first green disappears under nine thousand balls, all of disputed ownership?"

Percy paused, began to speak, paused again and finally said. "Excellent. Good one, Cuthbert. We need coloured balls. Well spotted, mate," and off he went in his turned-down wellies, considering all the possibilities.

Cuthbert watched him go and shook his head. Percy seemed completely at home with himself. Nothing was really a problem, only an opportunity.

An opportunity was a chance to solve an anomaly, and that wasn't a problem, either.

Chapter Thirteen

Henry surveyed the room. It was actually the bar, but being multi-functional to respect the community, today it was 'The Meeting Room'.

Around the table sat Ronald, the Captain and Jasper. The men had pints and Jasper had a grievance. Ronald was deliberately smacking his lips every time he sampled his pint and Jasper could only gaze solemnly at his orange juice.

Henry addressed the assembly in his measured ex-newscaster tones. "Gentlemen, we cannot possibly win this tournament. I have travelled the globe and played golf with some unlikely people in my time, but this team is a travesty. We need ideas, and we need them quickly."

He leant back in his chair and watched as Jasper took a breath and Ronald took a long draught from his glass.

With exquisite timing, Jasper announced, "We need two ringers for Cuthbert and Percy."

The magnificent head of froth from Ronald's pint glass exploded across the table and everyone leapt backwards. It was like a scene from a poker game at the last chance saloon.

Everyone settled down and Ronald recovered enough to splutter, "Ringers for those two? Is the circus in town?"

Jasper was pleased enough with his tactic. The suggestion had really been irrelevant, so he just shrugged.

Henry gave it a tiny amount of thought, just to be polite. "Not an easy one, Jasper. I still haven't worked Cuthbert out myself yet. And as for Percy ..." collective heads shook around the table in understanding, "... he is like some strange shape-shifter."

"I saw some of those in the jungles of Borneo," said Ronald. "Just when you think you know what he looks like, he changes."

The Captain came in with, "Just when you learn to ignore him, he comes out with a real gold nugget."

Henry added, "Yes and we have to sift through several tons of spoil to get to it, too."

The silence persisted to the point where it seemed a shame to disturb it, and gradually each of them nodded to the others and went their separate ways.

Ronald was giggling to himself and wringing stale beer from his tie. "Good grief, find another Cuthbert, eh?" and when the next thought came he had to lean on a wall to support himself. "Another Percy! Imagine a family of them. The 'Munsters' could run for president!"

He spotted the crow watching him carefully. At least he thought it was a crow; it was black.

The alcohol haze was very slightly short-circuiting his thought processes and he briefly wondered, if the crow turned white, would it still be a crow?

Would a sensible, golf playing Percy still be the same Percy they all knew? 'By Jove,' he thought, 'I've got it!' Fuelled by inspiration, Ronald spun on his heel and headed back to tell his brother.

The crow watched fascinated as Ronald tried to plait his legs and fell flat on his face.

One of life's phenomena which had always intrigued Ronald was the fact that whenever a drunk fell asleep outside, it was always below freezing when he woke up. No matter what time of year, or which country it happened in, it was always freezing.

Sat in front of the fire in the bar, with a blanket around his shoulders and a brandy clutched in his hands like a lifeline, he had at last stopped shivering. Now for the hard part.

Drunken inspiration was all very well but it never sounded the same when the blood stopped fizzing. Of course, convincing someone else who was sober was never easy either, but he was giving it his best shot.

Henry, Jasper and the Captain all exchanged glances. People had spent fortunes on seeking pirate treasure after conversations with convincing drunks. Religious grottoes had been established after nocturnal visitations on the way home from the pub.

Henry began. "So the idea is to transform Percy into a gentleman so that the ladies don't accept that he is Percy?"

Ronald nodded.

"Sounds like Pygmalion to me," scoffed the Captain.

"It's not pig muck," slurred Ronald angrily. "It could work."

Henry refrained from comment and looked at Jasper as if this was totally his fault. Jasper, for his part, was enthralled. "Reverse psychology," he whispered. "This is good. You don't get ideas like that on orange juice."

Henry judged his moment and asked, "Does this include Cuthbert?"

Ronald slumped. Stretching the credibility of an idea was always difficult, especially if it involved funding it out of someone else's pocket.

Somehow, involving Cuthbert in the same scheme as Percy seemed like 'One small step for man, one giant leap too far.'

Chapter Fourteen

Cuthbert and Percy sat on one side of the kitchen table. Henry, Ronald, the Captain and Jasper sat on the other.

It was reminiscent of the famous painting, 'When did you last see your Father?' But the questions today were difficult enough without that one.

Cuthbert and Percy glanced at each other. The morning had started well enough.

Percy had literally saved the bacon when a huge tongue of flame shot out of the kitchen range and cleared the ants' nest from under the table. Cuthbert had swung open the shutters and stunned an owl in the thatch.

Then came the knock at the door. Someone had once told Cuthbert that the world's shortest ghost story was, 'The last man alive on earth was eating alone when there was a knock on the door.'

Cuthbert thought that a knock on the door when you knew it was Percy was far more suitable, but this time they were in the same room as each other anyway.

The deputation had entered and sat opposite the pair, and they were smiling.

Now, Cuthbert knew for sure that visitors smiling was not good news. Words like, "Was that your tractor speeding through the village late last night?" or "Who did you say was buried in plot forty-seven because the recent floods have caused us to check the records?" were usually accompanied by these sorts of smiles.

Henry coughed and re-assumed the smile of a friendly inquisitor. "So you see, boys, the only hope we've got is to convince the ladies that you two are not who they think you are. In which case, they won't dare play against you in case they lose." Henry sat back, confident that the explanation was succinct enough for the job.

The Captain decided to fill the silence with, "A reverse Pygmalion, if you like." The silence deepened.

Percy tried, "Noilamgyp," gurning his way around the unusual word on offer.

Cuthbert stared at Henry. Jasper corrected the Captain. "No, it's the psychology that's reversed. Pygmalion is as it should be. Silk purses out of sows' ears." Cuthbert now stared at Jasper.

Percy seemed to be trying to set 'Noilamgyp' to music as he rolled it and repeated it to himself, frowning with concentration.

Cuthbert seemed to be staring at Henry and Jasper at the same time, which unnerved everyone.

Ronald wasn't sure whether to take credit for this or not yet, so he tried, "The rain in Spain stays mainly on the plane," inviting disturbing stares from Cuthbert and Percy together.

"No, it doesn't," stated Percy. "Gardeners' hell is Spain. Cactus, that's all they get." Ronald's jaw dropped open. Percy continued, "Palm trees everywhere. Place looks as if it's covered in broken umbrellas."

"Enough!" shouted Henry. We need to get this plan into operation and set the seeds of doubt among the women. Percy, Cuthbert, can you transform yourselves for a while to help us out?"

The next voice came from Percy's direction. It was Percy's face, it was under Percy's hat but the resemblance ended there.

"Gentlemen, let me introduce myself. My name is Wills, W.D. Wills. I am a member of the Senior Service. My office is on Park Drive, near Pall Mall, telephone number State Express 555. If I cannot be reached, please use my assistants, Benson and Hedges, to reach me. Should I be abroad, I will be using my nom de plume, Peter Stuyvesant."

The occupants of the room were transfixed. It was like being at a séance where someone was taken over by the conman behind the curtain.

Henry shook his head in admiration. "Only Percy could turn a list of cigarette companies into a speech."

All eyes swivelled towards Cuthbert. Cuthbert cleared his throat. Jasper stopped him instantly. "Sorry, Cuthbert," said Jasper, "that sounded just like Cuthbert."

Cuthbert fumed. Percy being smug was bad enough, but Percy being quietly smug was unbearable.

How was it that Percy spent his life being a blundering incompetent until there was a chance to make Cuthbert look small?

The whole idea stank. Even if they convinced the women that they were not the original Cuthbert and Percy, they would lose the match because they still couldn't play golf.

Chapter Fifteen

Cuthbert strolled over to the old cinema.

It should really be called the new theatre now, but people seemed to find it easier to remember what was instead of what is.

He strode through the huge foyer and entered the biggest room where the new stage had been built.

Somehow Cuthbert's furniture had once again been enrolled for stage props and he went over to the stack of old suitcases.

They were beautiful old things, covered in labels from foreign parts and gleaming softly with a smugness only old leather can muster.

The catches released with a nail-blackening clunk! Cuthbert peered inside the one on top of the pile. Opening another compartment in the lid, he removed a flat tin box of theatrical make-up. Scooping up various accessories, he headed purposefully towards the dressing rooms.

The Mandrake Arms had relaxed into its primary role of meeting place and drinking den and the conversation ebbed and flowed.

When the stranger entered, the conversation ebbed but the drink still flowed. The man was silhouetted in the doorway for a moment and when he stepped inside, he looked carefully around at his new surroundings before heading for the bar.

He wore a long coat, a hat and carried a cane. Stroking his moustache seemed to be a nervous habit and he cleared his throat before ordering a pint. Several people glanced his way and frowned thoughtfully.

Strangers didn't just wander into the Valley by accident and they certainly didn't see any 'Welcome' signs.

Constable Beeching and Blind Pugh made sure of that. A stranger usually sported a parking ticket and a limp. This man had a cane, but there was no trail of blood on the floor.

Margery had served the man, but failed to draw him out on anything other than his thirst. She looked at her husband Henry, with raised eyebrows.

Henry began to rise but his brother Ronald put a hand on his arm. "It's Cuthbert. Didn't you hear him clear his throat?" Henry paused and sat down again, looking at his brother in admiration.

Ronald continued, "Did anyone hear a car?" He looked around the table feeling intensely smug. "Where's his ticket, where's the blood? The little twerp is trying to impress us like Percy did. Even Blind Pugh would see through that disguise."

Heads nodded wisely around the table as Ronald stood. Sidling up to the bar, Ronald affected a nonchalant air as he began to make conversation. "Buried anyone interesting lately?" he began.

The man appeared momentarily startled and replied. "I'm sorry, I don't understand. You may have mistaken me for someone else."

Ronald gave his most dangerous smirk and continued, "So you are not the local undertaker and theatre impresario formerly known as Cuthbert?"

The man reluctantly turned to look at Ronald and replied, "Undertaker? Oh, I see, it's an allusion to my long coat and hat. Very droll, my man, very droll."

All attention was now focused on this gentle confrontation, but Ronald needed a result or the sniggers would begin. "Alright then, let's play a game," said Ronald. "You tell me who you think you are, and then I'll tell you why you're not."

The man looked about as annoyed as he was ever going to be as he replied," I, sir, am Sir Toby Topham and I have business here in the Valley."

Ronald mimicked the man's accent as he rejoined with, "Sir Toby Topham? What sort of cartoon name is that? Come on, Cuthbert, the jig's up. You could never pass yourself off as a toff, even if you look dozy enough!"

Behind them, Henry was beginning to wonder - the name sounded vaguely familiar - but Ronald ploughed on. "That's enough, Cuthbert - the funny hat, the funeral coat and a fake moustache. Talk about amateur theatricals. And that voice!"

'That voice' now took on a deeper tone as its owner scanned the room. "Is there a Henry Chisolm in the house?"

Henry began to stand, his suspicions now setting into rock-hard certainty. "I am Henry Chisolm," he said.

The man at the bar gave Ronald a last withering look and approached Henry. "I am the competition adjudicator. I have just walked over from the next valley to inspect the golf course."

Henry offered a handshake and was ignored. "Er, is everything in order?" stammered Henry.

The man smiled. In that smile was revenge for every slight he had ever suffered in life. He pulled out a map, laid it on the table and drew from his pocket a felt tip marker.

"This is the actual course," he said, tapping his pen against the map. The pen top came off with a pop! The man drew a random loop around the course, extending it by some distance. "This is the new designated course," he said smoothly. "Add another four holes, commit any prize monies to charity and the games may commence. Otherwise it will be judged that the other team wins." The man was actually getting used to smiling.

Sir Toby Topham swept out of the bar, briefly colliding with his 'Doppelganger' coming the other way. Neither of them noticed each other deep in their own thoughts. The crowd in the bar called out "Oh nice one, Ronald. Well done!"

The occupants of the bar began to leave by the back door just as Cuthbert entered with a cheery "What-ho, strangers, I am in need of refreshment!" Distracted by the empty room, he forgot his long coat and fell flat on his face, knocking over a table and burying his face in a map.

Ronald, the last man in the room said, "Oh nice one, Cuthbert. Well done!"

Cuthbert slid his soggy false moustache across the paper and wondered why someone had drawn a circle around his farm.

Chapter Sixteen

The ladies' meeting had been going quite well.

Arkle had been practising and reduced the power of her swing so that the balls weren't turning to dust when she hit them.

Margery had sorted out some revealing outfits which swung provocatively when she did. Elspeth, the Captain's wife, was in charge of refreshments as usual and an air of a win already accomplished hung in the air.

"Oh, excuse me, ladies," said Percy politely. "I must have the wrong meeting."

The ladies were startled. Everybody knew when Percy was approaching. You could hear the thump of his turned-down wellies before the smell of the garden arrived.

"The men have booked the bar for their losers' meeting," boomed Arkle, bringing smiles all round.

Percy smiled in return. "Competitive, that's the spirit," he said, "My, what is that perfume? It brings to mind a beautiful woman lounging in a Corsican citrus grove."

Margery blushed furiously and stammered helplessly.

Percy cast his monocle clad eye around the room. "Ah, Elspeth. May I call you Elspeth?"

The Captain's wife whispered, "Yes please, no-one else does," and cast her eyes down rapidly.

Arkle boomed into the room, "Don't come in here with your cheap tricks, Percy. We aren't to be swayed that easily."

Percy gazed at her fondly before stating, "Saw you ride past yesterday, my dear. Wonderful seat, dear girl. Magnificent filly."

Arkle's complexion turned to a beetroot colour and her jaw dropped. "Why, thank you ..." she began as Percy turned on his heel and left the room.

There was a long silence in the room. Avril had been sitting quietly in a corner compiling notes for the local paper, looking carefully around at the other women studiously avoiding each other's eyes. She ventured, "Well, you lot soon reverted to stereotype, didn't you? And with Percy of all people."

The women glanced around furtively until Margery had an inspiration. "That wasn't Percy!" She paused to collect her thoughts and continued. "In the bar, when Ronald thought that man was Cuthbert in disguise, he said, 'It's Cuthbert trying to impress us like Percy did'." She followed the thought with, "Either Percy is suddenly a damn good actoror it's a ringer!"

"What on earth is a ringer?" asked Elspeth.

"Good God, woman," barked Arkle. "Haven't you ever painted a horse so that it looks like another horse just before a race?"

"Er, no," replied Elspeth meekly.

"Oh!" said Arkle looking around wildly, "neither have I, but it's that sort of thing, apparently." She excused herself quickly and went outside to jump a few fences and settle down a bit.

"She didn't take her horse," noted Elspeth.

"So?" chorused the room.

Chapter Seventeen

Percy found the rest of the men in Cuthbert's kitchen. Faces were red and chairs were back against the wall.

Knuckles were resting on the table and veins were throbbing in foreheads. "Active debate, eh, chaps? Well done, well done," he said walking across the kitchen and tightening his monocle.

"What the blazes is that for?" asked Ronald.

Percy looked at him pityingly before replying, "It's toff's-wear, old boy. Marks out those with style."

Ronald leered at him and said, "We once had an officer who wore one of those in battle."

"Really?" asked Percy. "Did it help?"

"It helped us. When the sun glinted off it, we knew where to aim."

Percy absorbed this for a moment, removed the monocle for cleaning and left it dangling on his chest.

The argument continued.

Cuthbert was convinced that they had sold his farm to extend the golf course. Ronald was blaming everybody but himself and the Captain was reading Mrs. Beeton's Cookbook ready to start his life of servitude under the women.

Percy gave a subtle, "Ahem," but couldn't get anyone's attention. His next move was to kick open the cooking range door, releasing a tongue of flame across the room. That worked. The room settled and everyone sat down. Percy took command. "I don't see what the problem is," he began.

"The problem is that they have doubled the size of the course, you numbskull!" yelled Ronald.

Percy waited a moment and said, "Yes, but where have they extended it?"

"Around Cuthbert's farm," explained Henry patiently.

"Exactly," shouted Percy.

Cuthbert interrupted loudly. "See, Cuthbert's farm, my farm, that's why it's called Cuthbert's farm."

Percy continued. "Yes, they've extended it right across Cuthbert's pitch and putt course. How many of the women will be able to hole a ball the way Cuthbert does in his own back yard?" As he spoke, he seemed to be outlined by a haze giving him an ethereal quality. "Oh ye of little faith, why does no one take me seriously?" he asked.

"Because the sun shining through your monocle has set fire to your coat?" ventured Henry.

Chapter Eighteen

The new course was proving taxing for everyone.

It was miles to walk and the bags of clubs were dragging in the dirt by the halfway point.

Attempts to get the Valley Mafia involved as caddies failed miserably, because after a visit to the bookies in the next town, every one of them had a vested interest in one of the teams.

Henry seemed to be the only one fit enough to complete the course and he stood with his hands on his hips surveying his team. They lay about like extras from a disaster movie, limbs splayed in all directions and clubs scattered around like battlefield debris.

Percy lay gasping like a beached seal and Cuthbert was crawling along, pulling at the grass as if he could draw the hole closer. Ronald sat with his head between his knees muttering ineffectual curses to himself.

Henry waited until they could hear him over the sounds of their own breathing and said, "This won't do, it won't do at all. We need transport."

The idea settled in the dark regions of Percy's brain. It spread slowly as his breathing regulated and a curious tingling went all the way into his wellies. "Leave it to me," he said.

Cuthbert had never really hoarded; he just never threw anything away. The outbuildings of his farm were a treasure trove to Percy: boxes of stuff, shelves full of stuff and crates stuffed with stuff.

But the moment he would always remember was when he forced open an old stubborn door and saw it.

The miniature digger looked like a badly injured scorpion. Its arm and claw rested on the ground, the cab window hung open forlornly and it sat upon rusty caterpillar tracks. Percy was alive.

This would be the ultimate all-terrain golf buggy. He circled it, taking in every detail and rubbing an imaginary oily cloth between his hands.

Cuthbert followed closely, trying to explain that it wasn't really his. He had hired it from one of the big towns when some of the old tunnels collapsed and he had to retrieve several coffins from the depths.

He had re-interred them all and firmly insisted that they stay where they were put this time. The contractor had sent a young lad along to drive it back when Cuthbert had finished with it, but the young lad had become smitten by Mrs. Biggle's daughter who worked in the Post Office.

Needing more time to win her over, he started to invent 'mysterious happenings' and delays, anything to let him stay there for longer. He hinted at 'strange people and weird events.'

There was always some unforeseen disaster keeping him from accomplishing his mission. The last telephone call had been 'cut-off' mysteriously and it sounded as if the handset had been left dangling.

Eventually, the contractor became fed up with all this and came to see for himself. But by this time, the young lovers had eloped without telling a soul. The contractor had parked outside the Post Office and enquired after his young assistant.

He left quite shaken when the woman behind the counter burst into tears and threw things at him. Then he moved on to the address where the digger had been delivered and parked in Cuthbert's farmyard.

From there he went looking for the digger. Pausing to glance inside one of the outbuildings, he saw a row of coffins standing upright in the gloom. Backing away, he tripped over a headstone carelessly left in his path. Moving towards a large barn-like structure he stared in disbelief.

Two witches were leaning against the door sharing a cigarette. A third witch appeared and they all entered the structure after grinding the cigarette end into the ground.

Giving the barn a wide berth, the contractor spotted the arm of the digger above some shrubbery, but as he moved towards it, he heard a steady whining noise. The hairs stood up on the back of his neck as he looked around.

The noise was between him and the digger and as he moved closer, the whine became louder, followed by a scream and a scarecrow seemed to shoot up out of the ground before him.

The contractor ran for his life and never mentioned either the digger or the Valley again.

Meanwhile, behind him, Percy climbed out of the old collapsed grave with his home-made metal detector stuck to his steel toe-caps. Cursing his luck, he threw the thing away and limped off to the barn to join the witches in rehearsals for Cuthbert's 'Macbeth'.

Cuthbert finished the tale and Percy muttered, "So we've got squatters rights for a digger, then?" and started searching for tools and an oily rag.

Cuthbert wandered around the farm carrying out bits of maintenance here and there. He was careful to not quite finish several of the jobs, otherwise the place simply wouldn't look like a farm; a loose shutter here, a stripped down tractor there, that sort of thing.

The undertaking business was particularly slack lately. Either the fresh air was causing longevity or practising for the golf match meant that people were too busy to die.

Cuthbert didn't allow himself to wonder if the bodies were going elsewhere. After all it was tradition: born in the Valley, live in the Valley, buried in the Valley.

Wait for the floods and get washed into the next valley. They took better care of their cemeteries anyway.

A roaring noise from the barn drew Cuthbert's attention and black smoke started to seep out from under the door.

This usually meant that Percy was about to reveal the result of his day's labours. The barn doors crept open one by one. If there was human assistance, Cuthbert couldn't see it amongst the smoke, and as it was Percy involved, too much investigating wasn't a good idea.

Then the clanking began. It started with a single Clank!, then another, until the clanking was almost constant, something like a man on two metal legs running down a steel ramp to avoid a rolling metal ball.

Percy stormed out into the sunshine blinking like a mole amidst a flurry of squealing caterpillar tracks and clanking track-plates.

The tracks were throwing clods of farmyard high into the air behind the machine and redistributing the topography alarmingly.

Percy sat low between the tracks pulling on various levers as he advanced on Cuthbert with a curious fishtailing motion. Cuthbert had the feeling that whichever way he ran, Percy and his diabolical contraption would follow, so he stayed where he was.

It briefly crossed his mind that the undertaking business might be about to pick up, but he himself might not actually benefit!

Percy slewed to a halt sideways on to Cuthbert and pushed his cap back on his head. A huge grin broke out from amongst the hair, cap, dust and grease. "Well, what do you think?" he yelled over the apocalyptic noise.

Cuthbert paused, because if Percy didn't get the right amount of recognition, he would sulk for days.

Then it occurred to him that Percy couldn't hear a word, so he began an elaborate mime showing gasps of what could be taken for admiration and expressions of what appeared to be deep interest.

Percy was satisfied. Giving Cuthbert a thumbs-up, he clanked off down the farm track, plastering Cuthbert in carefully laid generations of farmyard.

"Well," muttered Cuthbert to himself. "If we did have a golf course, we won't have one after he's played the match on that thing."

Chapter Nineteen

Later that afternoon, Cuthbert heard a muffled thump! He looked towards his kitchen door, it was bulging inwards. Either all the little furry animals in the thatch had finally made the roof too heavy, or Constable Beeching was getting his breath back before the exertion of knocking.

The door flew open and Percy stamped in, neatly avoiding the outstretched arm of the officer stuck in the doorway. "Interfering busybody," he huffed as he negotiated all the obvious pitfalls of the cooking range and poured himself a cup of tea.

Cuthbert chewed thoughtfully at the turned-up edges of his cheese sandwich as the Constable twisted his way through the door frame and slumped onto a chair, gasping.

Percy sat opposite him and glared at the officer, waiting for him to regain his breath. Percy had been wearing an old pair of flying goggles and had pushed them up onto the front of his cap. This left two white patches around his eyes and made him look like a red-haired panda wearing a cap.

No-one spoke.

The Constable wheezed his way back to normality and took out his notebook. "Percy, I am arresting you for theft," he began.

Percy continued to glare at him.

Cuthbert sat upright. Now he knew what was going on and he began to intervene. "No, no, it's not what you think. Percy took it from my outbuilding and I knew all about it." Cuthbert sat back, content that he had cleared everything up.

Constable Beeching scribbled through the lines he had just written and said, "So, Cuthbert, you admit taking it in the first place, so that he could take it in the second place on his way to the third place? In that case, Cuthbert, I arrest you for theft."

Cuthbert stammered, "Er, I didn't take it. It was delivered to me."

Constable Beeching scribbled out his last words and began again, mumbling under his breath as he wrote, "The local thief, known as Percy, stole the item from the notorious receiver of stolen goods, Cuthbert, and was on his way to an unknown destination when he was skilfully apprehended by me."

Cuthbert just gaped, but Percy said sullenly, "You crashed into me. You shouldn't be eating pizza when driving on official business."

Constable Beeching lowered his notebook menacingly. "Is the prisoner making accusations? Can he substantiate any of them?"

Percy smirked. "Well, the pepperoni slices on your cheeks are a dead giveaway."

The Constable spluttered. "It is my duty to carry out consumer testing in the Valley to protect you ungrateful lot. Anyway, where you're going, there won't be any pizza or bridge."

Cuthbert scowled. "Percy doesn't play bridge" he said uncertainly.

The Constable looked him straight in the eye and asked, "Then what's that about to fall off the back of his lorry, then, eh?"

Cuthbert noted Percy's eyes shiftily swinging to the door and he stood up and looked outside. There, balanced across the back of Percy's new golf cart, was a steel bridge which until recently had spanned the main road out of the Valley. Behind it, a police car and two lines of severed trees stretched back down the Valley. Cuthbert returned to the table and sat down quietly. Percy and the Constable were watching him closely.

Cuthbert looked at Percy and said, "You stole a bridge?"

Percy looked sheepish as he replied, "I was going to give it back."

Constable Beeching muttered, "A likely story," and tried to reach behind his back for the handcuffs on his belt, which was like watching a dog slowly chasing its own tail. The chair legs squealed in protest each time he jerked further around and the handcuffs stayed the same distance away.

Cuthbert pulled himself away from this fascinating pantomime and asked Percy, "Why did you steal a bridge?"

Percy looked uncomfortable and replied, "I didn't mean to. I built a telescopic platform on the back so we could raise it during the game for a better view and maybe lob a few balls off it from a great height."

Giggling at his ingenuity, he continued, "Halfway out of the Valley, I decided to test it without realising that I was under the bridge." He glared at Cuthbert ready for a retort but Cuthbert had learnt patience.

He slipped his face into neutral to let the whole sorry saga reveal itself. Percy continued, "My goggles were steamed up and it was getting dark."

Cuthbert didn't have that much patience. "Yes, I can see where it could get dark under a bridge," he said without a flicker of expression.

Percy glared, but continued, "There is so much power in that thing, it lifted the bridge clean off. When I drove forward a bit to see what had happened, it just came with me." Percy nodded towards the slowly circling officer who was showing signs of getting dizzy now. "That's when Constable Colossus appeared. He ran straight into the back of me. After he'd peeled a giant pizza from his face, he asked me what I thought I was doing."

Percy fell silent, so Cuthbert prompted him, "And you said?"

Percy looked mildly pleased with himself as he answered. "I told him I was delivering it to the next valley."

Cuthbert's facial muscles groaned with the effort of staying neutral and he asked, "Did he believe you?"

Percy brightened. "Oh yes! He told me to be more careful where I parked and drove off."

Cuthbert was an old hand with Percy and he waited whilst Percy's memory of events flashed across his face before asking, "So what happened next?"

Percy split his face with a huge grin and said, "He drove up the slip road and tried to cross where the bridge had been. He landed slap bang back in front of me - twice!"

Cuthbert gave up and the pair of them collapsed laughing across the table.

Constable Beeching tried to change direction to see what all the fuss was about and fell off his chair. Inertia and gravity decided to arm wrestle for him at ground level and he passed out.

Percy added, "His car is actually tied to the back of the golf cart."

Cuthbert remarked, "So you were arrested by a man at the end of his tether?"

The pair collapsed across the table again.

Chapter Twenty

The pub was celebrating the return of Geraldine.

She had been the Museum Curator in the Valley when a lot of the adventures had begun. She had also been the only love interest to ever keep Cuthbert awake at night.

Arkle and Geraldine had departed the Valley to take part in worldwide archaeological digs. Arkle had returned home and sent for her to be part of the women's golf team.

When Percy and Cuthbert entered, she was regaling the room with tales of faraway places. The subject was 'Sky Burials'. Geraldine had described the wonder of the body laid on a high platform where the birds competed to distribute it amongst themselves as the shaman chanted and the sun rose.

Anywhere else, she could have dined out on her stories for months, but in the Valley she was met with Ronald saying, "Huh! I don't fancy coming back as bird-muck," and someone else muttering, "How would we tell?" This was followed by various shouts of, "That's Cuthbert out of a job, then."

Geraldine and Cuthbert smiled at each other and Ronald began trying to top the story with tales of his days in Borneo. "We had head-hunters out there. Every time they killed an enemy, the head was shrunk and hung from the lodge pole. Some had dozens of them, all with their mouths sewn shut." Ronald sat back to enjoy the horrified looks from the women.

Cuthbert asked, "Why sew the mouths shut? They wouldn't have much to say by that point."

Ronald glared back at him and muttered darkly, "You don't have to be dead for it to be sewn shut, mate."

Someone foolishly asked to hear more about Ronald and his world-taming adventures and he launched into a 'Boys' Own' list of intrepid adventures. At one point, he looked around the room and commented, "None of you here know what you've missed by not serving the flag."

Percy rose to the occasion. "My family has a long tradition of serving its country."

Ronald sneered. "What as, waiters?"

Percy ignored him and continued, "One of my ancestors was the drummer boy in charge of selecting Special Forces."

Most of Ronald's pint exploded across the table. His face turned red. "What a load of tosh. Drummer boy? How far are you going back? How the blazes can a drummer boy choose Special Forces?"

Percy shuffled until he was comfortable and explained. "Back in the days when the drummer boy tapped out the marching rhythm to keep everyone in step, it was his job to keep an eye on the ranks and weed out anyone not suitable. After he got rid of all the 'Two left feet' merchants and sent the 'knuckle-draggers' to the infantry, he was supposed to watch out for those with special abilities. He devised a method where he would unexpectedly change the marching rhythm and take everyone by surprise. Anyone who matched his steps to the beat, then performed a pirouette and recovered quickly, was highly suspect and made an Officer. The ones that were left were Special Forces."

Percy sat back, content with the attention as Henry, the Captain and Arkle were trying to wrestle Ronald to the floor and keep him from reaching Percy while there was some furniture left.

Chapter Twenty-One

The atmosphere in Cuthbert's kitchen was cosy.

The cooking range belched softly in the corner, somehow radiating heat and a sense of danger at the same time. Cuthbert and Percy sat opposite each other staring vaguely into their coffee mugs.

Percy broke the silence with, "So, Geraldine is back."

Cuthbert sighed and looked up. "Yes, but I think we are over each other. It felt like seeing an old friend. We never seemed to belong together somehow."

Percy took a noisy slurp and contributed, "Well, from what I saw, it was a matter of degree." He slurped again as Cuthbert paid attention. "She's got one and you haven't."

Cuthbert rose to the bait. "Are you saying that I'm not good enough for her?" Cuthbert was appalled. "I have a house, a career, and I run a theatre company." As if to pre-empt any comment from Percy, the old house gave a long groan as it settled into its foundations like a rheumatic old lion settling onto its haunches after giving up the chase.

Cuthbert was well aware that his funeral business was sorely lacking in any sort of profits. It was really difficult to squeeze a corpse for a bonus and relatives were always conveniently mourning.

The theatre company, of course, simply came with the territory. Cuthbert's mother had handed down the duty of performing plays by Shakespeare as a way to remind everyone that he may once, just possibly, perhaps have taught at the old Hall as a young man.

With ancient buildings and a network of underground tunnels and rumours of lost manuscripts, the Valley had intrigue coming out of its fissures, but somehow it held on to everything.

Even the glut of strangers and adventurers had now become residents and were slowly forgetting about the outside world. The Valley seemed to fold people into its embrace and cushion them from reality.

Cuthbert knew that he could never compete against the bearded men in shorts and sandals that Geraldine associated with. He couldn't even grow thick eyebrows, never mind a beard.

Percy was watching him, so Cuthbert tried the tactic of 'reverse inquisition'.

"Did you go to university Percy?" he asked.

Percy was taken by surprise. He stroked his chin, frowned and stroked his chin some more. The question obviously wasn't going away so he tried the 'reverse innuendo'. "Do you want me to have gone to university, Cuthbert? Would that give you an excuse to claim that you were prevented by hardship?"

Cuthbert gazed at Percy in amazement. "I only asked …"

Percy sat forward. "Of course you asked, the inadequate will always seize upon someone else's success and use it to justify their own meagre achievements."

Cuthbert spluttered, "But all I asked was …"

Percy pounced. "Yes, exactly. That's the point. You have proven the theory of 'Equivalent justification of one's own personal existence'." Percy sat back as he seemed to hold all the cards.

Cuthbert studied him for a moment before asking, "That's a no, then, is it?"

Percy gathered the cups and went to wash up. A mutual silence settled upon the scene.

Geraldine had brought everyone up to speed on her latest adventures and was hearing about the proposed match.

The five woman team would consist of herself, Margery, Arkle, Belinda the barmaid and Avril, who would also report the event for the local paper.

Margery had subtly enquired about any lingering romantic involvement with Cuthbert. No-one wanted sympathy of any kind to creep into this particular turf war.

Geraldine had counter enquired about the sympathy between Margery and her husband Henry. This had been greeted by gales of laughter and shouts of, "You've never been married, have you?"

The sherry flowed freely, and as there was no need at all to discuss tactics or strategy, the ladies resorted to making sure that no-one wore clashing outfits.

The men meanwhile needed another player. No-one ever invited Percy or Cuthbert to these meetings.

Somehow Cuthbert didn't give the discussion any forward momentum and Percy actually drove it backwards.

Henry stretched his arms above his head and stifled a yawn.

The Captain suddenly asked, "Whatever happened to that chap who always played the lead in Cuthbert's plays?"

Ronald was staring morosely at the floor. All these meetings did was to remind everybody that it was all his fault. "The milkman," he muttered.

"That's right, the milkman. Where did he go?" boomed the Captain.

Henry lowered his arms and looked very interested. "I forgot about him. Does anyone know where he is?"

Ronald looked up. "I know where his horse is. It frightened me to death sticking its head through my bedroom window yesterday."

After a few shrugs and murmurs, they realised that no-one had given the man a thought since he left the Valley.

Everyone promised to make enquiries and the party broke up, or it would have done if a shape at another table hadn't spoken. They all assumed that the shape had spoken, but no-one could be sure.

'Whistle' sat with his head down and his hood up, hunched over his pint as if the future was in the empty glass. As far as 'Whistle' was concerned it was.

Henry signalled to the barmaid to refill the offending glass and waited for 'Whistle' to lubricate whatever motivated his voice.

Entwhistle's hood raised itself slightly and he said, "What about Doctor Barnaby?"

Henry looked puzzled. "Doctor who?"

This provoked outbursts of "Diddly-dum-diddly-dum" as everyone gave their version of the theme tune. Henry couldn't resist smiling.

Entwhistle sighed as if he had heard that one before and repeated, "Doctor Barnaby. He plays golf"

The hood lowered itself again like an old fairground automata when the coin runs out and Henry looked around helplessly.

Everyone shrugged in return and Henry was reminded that they were still newcomers in the Valley. This was a matter for an urgent meeting of the full golf committee. All agreed to meet at Cuthbert's table the next morning and they wove their way home in different directions.

Chapter Twenty-Two

Out in the dark lanes, near the edge of the Valley, Cuthbert and Percy were manoeuvring the bridge back into position.

It was high in the air and almost lost against the night sky. Cuthbert handled the controls at the back to raise and lower the platform and Percy controlled the track movements.

The bridge clunked down into position but somehow it didn't sit properly. As Percy wrestled with the levers to spin the whole thing around, Cuthbert was fascinated by blue flashing lights approaching on the road above.

Unable to attract Percy's attention above all the noise, all he could do was watch as the phenomenon appeared on the bridge, turned with it and went back in the opposite direction as the noise died down with the engine turned off.

"Constable Colossal's pizza run," yelled Percy, jumping back onto the machine and firing up the engine.

For the next few hours they amused themselves by redirecting the speeding police car every time it drove onto the bridge.

Eventually, even Constable Beeching decided that fate was against him and gave up. Cuthbert and Percy clanked back to the farm with a sense of a night well spent.

Chapter Twenty-Three

A hammering on the farmhouse door was never good news, especially after a night spent directing traffic.

Cuthbert and Percy bumped into each other at the top of the stairs and again at the bottom.

Percy cautiously approached the cooking range and filled the kettle. Cuthbert was quite relieved to see that the door was not bending inwards from ConstableBeeching's weight, and curiosity overcame him as he opened the door.

The golf committee pushed in and Cuthbert found himself forced back against the edge of the table as a tide of questions threatened to engulf him.

"Where's the milkman?" and "Who is Doctor Barnaby?" with "Where's Whistle?" thrown in just to add to the confusion.

Cuthbert tried his famous goldfish expression as his brain was being press-ganged into action.

The questions did not stop. "Where's the milkman?" and "Who is Doctor Barnaby?" seemed to be the favourites.

Percy yawned and contributed, "Clark Kent is really Superman, if that helps."

The room went silent as everyone watched the back of Percy's head and Cuthbert edged away from the throng to sit at the end of the table.

Percy turned with a huge steaming kettle in his hands and waved it in the general direction of the table.

Everyone obediently sat as Percy started to pour a violent bubbling liquid into nearby cups.

"My Dad was a Doctor," he said. "Started as a gardener, tried growing watercress in the local lake but the manure kept floating away. Anyway, the upside was that after a few weeks he found that his wellies were full of leeches, so he set up as a Doctor instead.

Didn't last long, though. He had a terrible time getting people to swallow them."

As everyone looked around to try to ground themselves in reality, Percy finished pouring the tea and sat at the other end of the table, waiting patiently for someone to begin.

Henry roused himself. All the enthusiasm and demands had been defused by Percy's meandering and his voice was calm. "Cuthbert," he began, "who is Doctor Barnaby and why haven't we heard of him?"

Cuthbert looked around the table and asked, "Have any of you needed a poultice lately?"

The assembly gave a joint shudder. Memories of foul smelling concoctions from childhood came flooding back, a lump in a bandage with a faint green steam coming from it, wrapped around whatever ailed you and left to ferment until cured.

Cuthbert explained. "All he ever prescribes is a poultice. Always been the same. His wife made them up in a back room until she died. In fact she was covered in them when I buried her."

"Didn't work, then?" asked Ronald sarcastically.

"Oh, they worked well enough on the living, but she had been dead for days. He simply didn't notice."

Cuthbert sipped his tea as the Captain asked, "Does he play golf?"

Cuthbert thought for a while and replied, "I don't know. He is not very sociable. He puts 'Lord' into every sentence, 'Lord' this' and 'Lord' that'."

Henry asked, "Is he religious?"

Cuthbert sipped again. "If he was, he cured it with a poultice."

The next topic was the milkman. Some people remembered him leaving the Valley to seek his fortune after some foreigner conned everyone into buying milk in cardboard boxes. Cuthbert suddenly had a memory flash. "Percy, didn't you promise to look after his horse?"

Percy's eyes widened and with a quick "Ooops!" he left by the back door.

Chapter Twenty-Four

The meeting had adjourned, with Cuthbert being delegated with the task of approaching Doctor Barnaby.

The Doctor had an office above the Post Office. The lack of a sign outside meant that new patients couldn't find him and the steep stairs kept the lame at bay.

The stairs were always in darkness. The Doctor was notoriously mean. He only put a battery in his clock when he needed the time.

Cuthbert pushed open the door. A smell very similar to embalming fluid greeted him and he entered the empty waiting room. Even the chairs seemed to have slumped into a melancholy stance through the years of neglect.

Cuthbert blew the dust from a pile of magazines and flicked through 'Organic Poultry'. Cuthbert remembered this. The old receptionist had thought it said 'Organic Poultice' and had added it to the Doctor's library.

It had been a risky business with strange consequences. After the first patient left with a chicken around his neck, the waiting room had cleared and stayed clear for months.

Cuthbert realised that without there being a receptionist he was going to have to introduce himself. He opened the door to the Doctor's office, coughed politely and entered.

Now the Doctor had never been blessed with good hearing, but a symptom never escaped him. "Lord, nasty cough, that. I recognise that cough. How is that lad of yours? Cuthbert, was it? How's the wife?" Cuthbert eased himself carefully into an old captain's chair opposite the desk and promptly started to turn clockwise thanks to a broken bearing and a sloping floor.

"Actually, I'm Cuthbert, Doctor. My parents have been gone for some time now."

The Doctor peered at him with bright little eyes, the eyes of someone on someone else's medication. "Oh Lord, yes, I remember. Didn't some damn fool shoot him or something?"

Cuthbert struggled to turn the chair back so that he faced the Doctor again. "Yes, sounds about right," said Cuthbert, starting another orbit.

The Doctor went into professional mode and began to write out the prescription for a poultice. "Lord, soon clear that cough, Clothbert. This works every time." He paused from scribbling furiously and sighed. "Lord, victim of my own success, you know, Clothears. Lord, poultices are so good that no-one needs me anymore." He ripped the paper from the top of the pad and posted it into a slot in the wall. "Lord, pick the thing up on the way out. That woman will have it ready by then".

Cuthbert was gently circling in his chair as he saw the prescription float away outside on the breeze.

He also saw Percy's hat bounce past, and as he was on the first floor, he could only assume that his friend had retrieved the milkman's horse. "Er, thank you Doctor, but I had a personal errand in mind when I came in," began Cuthbert, broaching the subject of his visit.

He had discovered that if he let the chair circle, it was easier to talk each time he and the Doctor were face-to-face.

The Doctor sat back. "Oh Lord, one of those visits, eh? Well spit it out, man. It's all been said in this room. These walls don't have ears. Well, except for his, anyway," he added, nodding to a mounted stag's head on the far wall.

Cuthbert began. "Well, it's the talk of the village that you play golf and we're in trouble. We may need you on the course".

The Doctor sat up straight. "In trouble? Lord, intercourse? Typical of this Valley, at it like rabbits. Lord, sit still, man. You always were a fidget." The Doctor began writing furiously again. "Lord, one poultice for you, wrap it around twice a day, and one for her to sit on. Lord, then one for after the baby comes and then another for, Lord ..."

Cuthbert gave up. He stood up as the chair slowed down on the upgrade and made his way to the door with motion sickness plaiting his legs as he went.

Outside, he walked through a blizzard of prescriptions and watched Percy trot past hanging underneath a horse.

"How did you get on?" shouted Percy.

"Apparently, I'm pregnant," replied Cuthbert.

"Oh," said Percy as he trotted past.

Chapter Twenty-Five

Ronald was scathing about Cuthbert's attempt to recruit the Doctor.

Any chance to criticise someone else helped to deflect the blame from him. He ended his tirade with, "Send a boy to do a man's job. Always do it yourself," and left the pub to begin his mission.

As the man who had personally tamed all the darkest corners of the world, what was there to fear?

The rest of the golf committee slumped around the table politely, leaving Cuthbert alone with his abject failure.

Margery stood behind the bar cleaning glasses and listening to every word for snippets of strategy. She also provided a running commentary on the whereabouts of Percy, who tended to wander past from time to time in various attitudes of mounted and dismounted as the horse explored the village.

The saloon bar door crashed open and Ronald threw himself to the floor under one of the tables. He then slithered panther style across to the wall where he oozed upwards, flat against the wallpaper and undulated towards a far corner like a ninja truant.

Cuthbert raised an eyebrow and looked at Henry for guidance.

Henry shrugged and said, "Something's happened. He's gone tactical."

Margery announced, "Percy's outside. Now he's not."

In the far corner a slurping sound came from under 'Whistle's' hood as he dredged the bottom of his glass.

A companionable silence descended over the bar. Sometimes circumstances can be overwhelming and it's best to ignore them.

Eventually the Captain spoke. "What on earth is this contraption that Percy has been clanking about in?"

Cuthbert roused himself and explained to everyone that with the course being extended, the golf bags would be incredibly heavy and everyone would be exhausted by the time the game reached Cuthbert's farmyard.

Margery had been dragging her finger around the rim of a wine glass to make an eerie wailing sound. The sound stopped and everyone noticed.

Henry put his finger to his lips and then tapped one of his ears. He then indicated both of his eyes with two fingers of one hand and pointed back towards the bar where his wife was now desperately trying to make the same noise again as if nothing had happened.

Everyone in the room seemed to have military experience of some sort and they all understood these clandestine signals, all except Cuthbert. Cuthbert needed things said very clearly and preferably very slowly.

All the others nodded wisely and began to finish their drinks in an overtly casual manner. Then, one by one, they stood, yawned and wandered outside.

Cuthbert sat there bemused until Ronald re-appeared, grabbed him by the scruff of his neck and dragged him outside to join the others. Cuthbert understood; that was clear enough even for him.

Margery cursed softly. She had blown her cover but that twerp Percy had the right idea. The women would never manage to carry that lot around the new course. The men had an advantage ... for now!

Outside, the men grouped together. Not just out of solidarity, but because a large horse was thundering towards them with Percy running alongside, barely holding onto its mane as the animal's huge feet thrashed around very close to him as it galloped past.

"Can someone sort him out?" asked Henry. "We need a strategy meeting."

Ronald slipped his hand inside his coat and assumed a combat stance until Henry cuffed him around the ear and said, "Not like that."

Ronald sulked, the others mostly scratched their heads but the Captain looked around eagerly.

Outside the pub was a pyramid of coconut shells, a kind of memorial to an earlier battle fought and won in the Valley.

The Captain broke two of them in half and stepped into the road. Tensing his shoulder muscles dramatically, he began to beat them together in a rhythmic tattoo. At the end of the street, the horse whirled around on its axis, flinging Percy into the horse trough. The Captain, having convinced the horse that another horse was challenging its authority, hid the shells behind his back and walked on whistling in a carefree manner.

The horse cantered past, eyes ablaze and headed out of the village in the opposite direction. The Captain returned the shells to the pile, and noticing the slack-jawed looks he was receiving, explained, "Little trick I picked up in the native mounted rifles regiment. We had to let them roam to find enough fodder. That was the way to bring them back in." He scratched his chin thoughtfully. "Stopping them was the real task though. Lost a lot of good men that way. Still, promotion came quickly out there."

Percy sat fuming in the horse trough. His little legs hung out over each side and his wellies were smoking.

"Managed to get off, then?" asked Cuthbert cheerily.

Percy wriggled free and flopped onto the ground like a landed cod. All he could do was trudge and squelch behind the others as they headed for the park.

Once at the park, Percy checked the litter bin and everyone else found a seat.

Ronald seemed twitchy and Percy noticed. Percy could always tell when a secret was desperate to stay hidden, or a scab needed to be scratched.

Ronald was downright shifty and looked around him constantly. If Percy was good at watching people, Cuthbert was good at watching Percy. He saw all the signs and knew how to exploit them, as the others had a quick swing or see-saw, just to get comfortable, you understand.

Cuthbert spoke. "While you were out riding, Percy, Ronald went in to recruit the Doctor."

Ronald's eyes lit up with malice and Percy's lit up with glee. "How did you get on, then?" asked Percy in all feigned innocence.

"Not well," he murmured.

"You're not pregnant as well, are you?" asked Percy solicitously.

Ronald had everyone's full attention. There was no escape. With one last glare at Cuthbert and a last check of his surroundings, he explained. "When I got there, I had the feeling that I had seen him somewhere before, but the chair started turning and distracted me. Suddenly, when I had my back to him, he yelled something about 'feeling a little prick' and injected something into the back of my neck." To emphasise the point he rubbed furiously at the spot.

Percy was in pursuit. "So, he definitely knew you, then?" he asked with glee.

Ronald glared but continued. "Many years ago we were sent to guard the diamond mines and keep out rebel insurgents. He was the medical officer at the mine."

There was more vigorous neck rubbing as the memories were shuffled into place. "We took cases of medical supplies in with us and risked our necks parachuting into the jungle with all this gear."

He said defensively, "The pay was never that good and we always had various schemes going for the retirement fund. Before we got to the mine we opened the cases and sold most of the supplies to the rebels which left us with several empty cases. So, we opened all the survival packs and repacked them with bicarbonate of soda. Nobody could tell the difference."

He paused to smirk at his ingenuity. "Anyway, we arrived at the mine, delivered the goods and set up the perimeter. There was no real threat because the rebels were full of happy pills and falling down tablets. It wasn't long, though, before the native workers were queuing up at the Doc's for various ailments and fractures and the new stuff was being handed out.

Suddenly the man had a strange epidemic on his hands. People were bloated and red in the face and no work was being done. This Doctor launched an investigation, shut down the mine and quarantined everybody. He sent telegrams all over the world announcing that he had discovered a new disease.

He called it 'Mal-de Rubicon Diamante' or something, I forget now. Anyway, the mine owners were screaming about lost revenue, the shareholders were in an uproar and the price of diamonds was going off the scale due to shortages. Then the rebels came knocking at the gates. It was obvious that the happy pills had run out and the falling down tablets interfered with rebellions something cruel. The spotlight fell on the Doctor. His paper on the new medical condition was ridiculed, the mine owners sacked him and he was chased into the jungle by the rebels."

Only the creak of ageing men on swings could be heard in the park until Henry asked, "So, basically, the man whose career and livelihood you destroyed and caused to be chased halfway around the world has just injected something into the back of your neck?"

Ronald rubbed the back of his neck nervously and replied, "Er …
yes."

Cuthbert glanced at Percy and saw the same spark reflected back
at him. Percy began the questions. "Ronald, are you growing breasts?"
Ronald's eyes widened.

Cuthbert came in with, "I thought his hair had grown but I was
distracted by him walking funny."

Percy continued with, "Now we need two more men for our team."

Ronald could stand no more. He clenched his fists and stormed, in
an exaggeratedly masculine way, out of the park. Behind him, there
was a squelch as Percy fell off his swing.

Chapter Twenty-Six

The women were alarmed. They had met up to have a leisurely knockabout and a gossip, but Margery had repeated the things she had overheard in the bar.

The conclusion was obvious; regardless of skill and low cut tops, the women would be exhausted halfway around the course.

Arkle was unfazed. "Can't see the problem personally," she said as she lifted her bag and marched away.

Margery looked after her sheepishly and said, "Er, you've got my bag there as well."

A wide-eyed Avril joined in with, "Mine too."

But Arkle was already out of earshot, so the others shared out the rest of the clubs between them and dawdled after her. It was all true.

The ladies would never cover the distance with all this gear, so by the fifth hole, they called for a conference halt. The only solution was to come up with their own transport. Everything was postponed for the day.

The women went home and turned out their sheds, garages and attics. The afternoon meeting revealed a motley collection of wheeled contrivances.

Margery had found a brewery trolley in the cellar of the Mandrake Arms. It weighed as much as a bag of golf clubs but at least it had wheels.

Geraldine had found an old baby's pram with incredible suspension in the Museum basement and all the others bowed to their instincts and bent to look inside with silly grins on their faces.

Belinda, the barmaid had been beaten to the brewery cart and was relying on her plunging neckline and doe eyes to get her through.

Avril had raided the newspaper office and borrowed an electric cart used by railway porters. It had a strange swivelling handle to steer it with, but at the squeeze of the handle, it was off! Avril was the hero of the moment until Arkle appeared.

Arkle was sitting astride an equally fearsome beast in the shape of her horse. It in turn was pulling a farm cart with high sides used to bring in the harvest.

The ladies were smitten. "A hay ride!" they chorused and all climbed aboard for a trial run.

Avril sat on the back watching her electric cart fade into the past, her moment of glory left behind with it.

The day was a raging success. The women covered the distance needed and still had enough high spirits left to ride through town and pelt the men with old soil clods from the back of the cart.

The men were not amused. The Captain considered it "Downright childish" and wondered if his tea would be late. Cuthbert was spitting out old straw and soil, and Percy was hiding behind him.

Ronald caught himself wondering if Belinda's lipstick was actually coral or blush pink.

It was Henry's turn to try and recruit the Doctor for the golf tournament. He wasn't really afraid.

After all, he had covered wars from some of the best hotels in the world and he once had a woman as his producer.

Henry climbed the stairs and was gasping slightly as he entered the Doctor's room. "I think you had better check my blood pressure after that," he half-joked.

The Doctor barked, "Lord, man, what do you think the stairs are for?" Henry studied the now notorious chair and remained standing.

The Doctor continued, "If you survive the stairs there's nothing wrong that a good hot poultice won't cure." He looked closely at Henry. "Lord, who are you, anyway? Outsiders aren't supposed to know about me!"

Henry stealthily looked around the room, his reporter's instincts returning. The room didn't seem to have any corners. There were books and documents stacked around the outer edges until the room became the inside of a circle.

"Well?" barked the Doctor, "Lord, what do you want? Boil on your bum? Is that why you can't sit down?"

Henry pulled himself together. "Do you play golf at all?" he asked.

The Doctor stared and started to write out a prescription. "Lord, I see, sports injury, eh? Trouble with one of your balls, eh? Just come out and say it, man. We are all men of the world, although some of us have seen more of it than we expected."

Henry remembered his brother's tale and decided that an alias might be a good idea.

The Doctor finished writing and posted the paper in the slot. "Wrap that around the offending area and leave for six months." Henry opened his mouth to re-open communications, but the Doctor bellowed, "Next!" and Henry found himself on the street.

The rest of the golf team sat on the edge of the horse trough waiting for him. Was Ronald sitting on a handkerchief, he wondered briefly.

The others picked out the defeat in his face and they all trooped off to the Mandrake Arms together.

As the drinks were placed before them, Cuthbert chose his moment and announced, "Must be your turn now, Percy."

Percy's eyes shot open in panic. "My turn? I don't carry money. Like royalty, me," he spluttered.

Cuthbert cut him off. "Not that. It's your turn to recruit the Doctor."

"Oh," said Percy, not sure whether he had come out of that well or not.

Percy had been gone some time. Each of the team took turns in watching from the door; no Percy and no prescriptions flying past.

"Been a long time," began Cuthbert.

"Probably driven each other nuts," muttered Ronald.

Several drinks later, Henry announced, "He's coming." They all crowded into the doorway and then crowded back out to let him in.

Percy took his seat and the questions began. "Any luck?" from Cuthbert.

"Any prescriptions?" from Henry

Followed by, "Any injections?" from Ronald

Percy took a long drink and enjoyed the attention. "Had a hard life, that one," he began. "Apparently, his parents took him to the Doctor's when he was young because he was always cold. The Doctor said that he was born with a layer of skin missing. He felt the cold that much that he always wore three pairs of underpants and two vests. That's why he went to work in the jungle where it was warm. But it seems that just as he was about to solve this problem for mankind, some bloke calling himself 'Chopper Chisolm' appeared and wrecked

67

his career. He spent eight months getting out of the jungle and has never been the same since."

The assembly was in awe. "How did you find out all this, Percy?" asked Henry. "I'm a professional and he wouldn't talk to me."

"How did you do it?" Ronald muttered. "Takes one to know one."

Everyone seemed to have missed the point, until Cuthbert asked, "Well, does he play golf?"

Percy took a long drink before replying. "He did. Apparently, he was world class until he was lost in the jungle. Didn't any of you notice that he is a bit short?" They all looked at each other and silently shook their heads. Percy snorted, "He hasn't got any legs. A crocodile got one and he had to eat the other one to survive."

All eyes swivelled towards Ronald. This golf tournament was not turning out to be his finest moment.

Chapter Twenty-Seven

The crow hopped across the stiff, short grass. He had caught a movement out of the corner of his eye. Something had just taken refuge in that hole.

Hopping over, he balanced on the edge and cocked his head from side to side. However designed, birds like this should have to live with his stiff neck.

The thing in the hole looked like one of those delicious 'fat-balls' that people hung out for the various tits. Why anyone wanted to encourage those noisy little twerps was beyond him.

Still he thought, 'While the tits are away the crow will play' and plunged his beak into the ball. The first two attempts bounced right off. 'Hmm', thought the crow, 'no wonder those little varmints have to hang on and peck like fury.'

Opening his beak to its full extent didn't work either; he just got wedged into the sides of the hole. The crow watched his prey with first one eye and then the other. It seemed unaffected by his killer stare.

This was it, then. The head came back and prepared itself with two practice dips before a lightning strike succeeded in piercing the outer layer.

The crow heaved the ball out of the hole and stared cross-eyed at his triumph. It was heavier than he expected and he didn't notice the thud of approaching footsteps.

A huge shadow fell across the scene, but all the crow could see was a white sphere before him wherever he turned. He was too top heavy to take off and a sense of impending doom began to nudge him.

The whoosh of the club just preceded the clack of contact and the crow felt the bones in his skeleton separate before they all rushed back together again.

His cheek feathers were wobbling with the speed and the trail of feathers made him look like Halley's Comet in silhouette.

On the ground, Margery looked skywards, shading her eyes as Arkle completed her swing. "Oh well done, dear!" she said. "Was that an eagle or a birdie?"

Chapter Twenty-Eight

Once again the old farmhouse table was witnessing history. The court of King Cuthbert was in session again.

Although far from the tense activity of the romantic court of Camelot, this table actually seemed to be hosting a discussion about lethargy.

Ronald was slumped to one side, Percy was rummaging through his pockets intently, and the Captain and Cuthbert were watching each other waiting for Henry. In fact, Cuthbert noticed, they both seemed to wait for Henry in exactly the same way.

The door opened and Henry seemed to bring some life into the room. Ronald sat up straight, Percy gave up his search, and the Captain and Cuthbert narrowed their eyes wondering what the other chap was staring at.

Henry bounded around the table and placed something in front of each of them. It landed with a click and seemed to be a flat square of plastic.

Cuthbert and Percy looked at the object and then at each other. Neither of them dared touch the thing. They had both heard about a 'Dead man's hand' in poker or the dreaded Black Spot of 'Treasure Island'.

Henry was saying that he had pre-programmed all their numbers into these mobile phones so that a meeting could be called at any time.

The Captain and Ronald flipped open their phones and examined them before putting them into their pockets. Percy nudged his with the end of his finger. It moved!

Ronald slid from the table and secretly called Percy on speed dial. The phone in front of Percy started to shake gently and then vibrate towards him. Percy watched in horror as it approached, and when 'The Ride of the Valkyries' boomed out of it, he ran.

Ronald really enjoyed that one and he surreptitiously watched Cuthbert reaching gingerly for his new toy. The two more mature members of the group shook their heads but couldn't resist watching Cuthbert.

The phone was in his hand and then the top flipped up. This was the nearest Cuthbert had been to technology and he felt a small thrill.

Then he realised that the thrill was travelling up his arm! Next, there was the crash of broken glass. Cuthbert went under the table and the phone bounced shut above him. Ronald's sides were hurting. Whoever had set these ring tones was a genius.

Henry volunteered to sit the pair of them down for a crash course in modern frustration and Ronald was sent away, well pleased with his day, to be labelled a 'distractive nuisance' at his age was quite an achievement.

The hours passed slowly. The kitchen was lit by sudden flashes as Percy took another photo of his ear. Cuthbert had changed his ring tone to a buzzing noise, and every time it rang, Percy batted away imaginary bees. But eventually, just ahead of Henry's nervous breakdown, things seemed to come together.

Cuthbert successfully contacted Ronald, and using a funny voice, sold him some land in the next valley, and Percy was seen striding up and down outside engaged in a furious discussion with someone.

Henry intercepted and discovered that it was a recorded message telling Percy that he had run out of talk-time.

Percy sheepishly admitted that he thought he was buying some of the land Cuthbert had just sold in the next valley.

By the time Henry left and Cuthbert closed the old house down for the night, his phone was by the bed. Percy's was tucked safely inside his welly.

Margery had the privilege of seeing the effects of modern life on the Valley the next day.

A mobile phone chirruped somewhere in the bar and everyone reached into their inside pocket like Secret Service men hearing a car back-fire.

Percy, true to form, reached into his welly and came out with a turnip.

Chapter Twenty-Nine

Cuthbert was alone in the theatre. It had seemed the answer to his dreams to have a building like this to stage the plays, but the golf competition had taken up the Valley's enthusiasm.

There had never been very much to go round in the first place. He supposed the problem was that all the newcomers had diluted the sense of tradition. The golf had taken over everything.

He had even seen the crow dragging a ball around in its beak. It seemed to be getting thinner these days; probably all that exercise. The crow dragged the white sphere for another two steps.

If he shuffled sideways, he could see the groove he had made all the way across the farmyard.

The crow had approached all the animals for help and had come to realise what a useless bunch they were.

Cows were cows and sheep were sheep; nobody expected much from them and they weren't disappointed.

But the birds, they twittered and chirped about how big they were and how much land they owned from the crack of dawn to last thing at night.

Big stupid pigeons could eat all day and carry out eighteenth century hopping dances when mating but were they any help? No!

The only one who had approached him had been a female crow who thought it was a stunt and she would be on the news. She soon left when she realised that he wasn't very good company with a beak full of golf ball.

He tugged at his burden and dreamt about worms and grubs and peanuts. If he didn't eat soon, the role would reverse and the golf ball would have a bit of beak stuck to it.

His target was just over the stile. If he could reach that noisy, smoking contraption the short scruffy one drove about in, he could wedge the ball into the machinery and it would pull free. Hah! 'If crows wore clothes they could rule the world,' he thought.

The crow leapt backwards onto the first step of the stile with great difficulty and it took even more effort to lift the ball onto the step beside it. One more step to go. This would go down in the annals of great crowdom, it would be told to chicks in nests all over the world.

He would be known as 'The crow who never gave up'. With a last heave, the ball reached the top and landed on a piece of bread. Oh the torment! That white fluffy texture, what would it taste like? 'Hang on a minute,' thought the crow, 'what's it doing there?'

Percy sat swinging his legs on top of the stile. He reached down for another hard-boiled egg and just as his lips closed over it he came face-to-face with the crow.

Cuthbert just happened to be leaning out of an upstairs window trimming the thatch when he thought he saw Percy running round in circles with a crow on his nose. The thatch was forgotten as Cuthbert grabbed his new phone and prepared to take a picture.

If a picture was indeed worth a thousand words, then a film of Percy and a crow trying to eat each other should run into volumes.

He snapped the phone open and activated the camera. Tripping over the window ledge in his haste, he found himself hanging upside-down staring at an inverted Avril.

Her eyes widened in horror as she screamed, "Are you filming down my blouse?" With a mighty slap which left Cuthbert swinging like a pendulum, she stormed off, back the way she had come.

Percy was tugging furiously at the crow. He wasn't giving up his boiled egg that easily. The crow was tugging wildly to get free and Cuthbert swung gently to a stop.

The crow, the ball and Percy parted company. The crow left to bury its face in the slice of bread as Percy munched away contentedly. Cuthbert fell out of the window. The farmyard returned to whatever passed for normality around here and the birds sang.

The next meeting involved the whole Valley and was held in the theatre.

Cuthbert noticed that all the women now had mobile phones; tiny little pink things. Mrs. Biggle was akin to Cuthbert with technology and had a habit of shouting into her powder compact and covering everyone in 'Skin Bliss', powder designed to reduce both your age and your bank balance, but not necessarily at the same rate.

Cuthbert had welcomed everyone to the meeting. He had also thanked everyone for coming to the meeting. He then proceeded to point out places of interest around the meeting, all in an attempt to remember why he had actually called the meeting. He still wasn't comfortable with people staring at him and expecting results.

Henry stood and smoothly took over. He explained that in view of the golf tournament, several members thought it might be too risky to stage 'The Taming of the Shrew', especially as poor Petruchio "gets knocked about a bit." The women listened stony-faced.

These plays were actually the highlight of the Valley's year. All the women got the chance to dress in the marvellous clothes of Shakespeare's England.

Henry could tell that this would need some selling.
Personally, he was very nervous about two rival factions carrying swords, unless as he joked, "It was the Montagues and the Capulets, but then that wouldn't be 'The Taming of the Shrew', would it?"

The attempt at humour failed miserably and only the chirp of a mobile phone and a cloud of dust from Mrs. Biggle gave him the opportunity to sit down.

Henry nodded at Percy to take over and the game little chap duly took centre stage. He started to speak, but Ronald speed-dialled him and caused his welly to vibrate. This produced a pantomime of hopping on one leg to retrieve his phone.

Next, Ronald dialled Cuthbert and this started Percy simultaneously to be hopping on one leg and swatting imaginary bees.

The audience looked on enthralled until someone shouted, "It's a film," someone else shouted and, "It's a book." The audience was soon on its feet shouting out suggestions.

"Hopalong Cassidy," shouted one.

"The Birds, idiot!" shouted another.

"Where's Welly?" cried a toddler.

Amongst the chaos someone admitted to being an alcoholic and someone else connected to the one who called him an idiot.

The auditorium was a seething, fighting mass, interspersed by clouds of powder as Mrs. Biggle tried to call the police.

Cuthbert, Henry and the Captain dragged Percy off the stage and they made their way out of the back. "I hope that sorted things out for you lads," said Percy.

Chapter Thirty

The women all met the next day. They commandeered the bar at the Mandrake Arms and made sure that no male bar staff were in attendance.

Geraldine had been busy helping out in her old job at the museum and hadn't been at the meeting last night, so she was puzzled as to why several of the women looked a bit worse for wear; one even had a black eye. The meetings hadn't been that exciting when she lived in the Valley.

Feelings ran high at the start; everyone wanted to defend tradition and, above all, wear the frocks. Gradually, the passion decreased as isolated voices pointed out that, "It really was a lot of trouble," and "Who gets the job of ironing and mending all those dresses, then?" The debate simply died a natural death and the women decided to concentrate on the tournament this year instead.

Geraldine stood and coughed politely to get everyone's attention. "Sorry I have missed so many meetings," she began, "but promoting museum projects around the world, I have made some interesting connections. I could put together a media deal to televise the match and arrange sponsorship for better equipment - clubs, bags, even proper golf carts, if you like. Obviously, it would be awful if the men were utterly humiliated worldwide, but there has to be a loser in every competition, eh, girls?"

The room began to buzz and this time it was nothing to do with Cuthbert's phone.

"Hats and shoes?" asked someone.

"More than likely," replied Geraldine.

"Photos in glossy magazines?" asked another.

"Guaranteed," grinned Geraldine.

"Films, books and plays?" added another.

The enthusiasm mounted, but stalled slightly as an excited Margery asked, "After the event orgies and show-biz scandals?"

Geraldine paused, and everyone held their breath. "Can't guarantee that one, I'm afraid."

Everyone exhaled. Geraldine was given free rein to check this out and the women took the excited hubbub home with them.

Cuthbert was outside practising on his make-shift pitch and putt course.

On the stile sat Entwhistle, or 'Whistle' as he was known locally.

Cuthbert looked at the cowled figure in amazement. He had never visited here before. He usually spent his time either in the pub or fishing in the empty reservoir.

Over by the barn, Percy seemed to be doing some kind of yoga exercises. He appeared to be firmly rooted to the spot and reaching slowly in all directions to stretch his muscles ready for the game.

It was only after Percy missed dinner that Cuthbert discovered that his friend had been tinkering with the tracked golf buggy and the exhaust flame had welded his welly to a metal plate.

Cuthbert approached the silent figure on the stile and peered into the front of 'Whistle's' hood. "Didn't expect to see you here," said Cuthbert. "Everything alright?"

The hood lifted slightly and Cuthbert heard, "Whistle see, won't we?"

"Whistle we?" asked Cuthbert, confusing himself almost immediately.

The opening in the hood spoke again. "I hear that you need another player, Cuthbert?"

Cuthbert stood back and re-appraised the figure before him. "I didn't know that you played golf," he exclaimed eagerly.

A snorting sound came from the hood. "No time for that nonsense. The fish won't catch themselves, will they?"

"Not in an empty reservoir, they won't," thought Cuthbert, but kept it to himself.

The voice continued, "I know someone who can help you." Cuthbert leaned in closer as 'Whistle' explained himself. He then shambled off up the hill so that the fish wouldn't be left twiddling their fins with nothing to do.

Later, when Cuthbert had released Percy and shown him the ruins of his dinner, and they had tried counting the gravy rings to see if it was possible to date a meal, Cuthbert gave Percy a few minutes to cut his gravy into slices and then told him about the visit from 'Whistle'.

Percy was wondering if he could repair his melted welly with the gravy and simply muttered, "Oh, right. What's the word from the hood?"

Henry was suspicious. "Walk out into the woods in the middle of the night to meet a mysterious stranger?" he said. "I am suspicious," he added. In the end a compromise was reached.

Ronald had always considered himself to be a Rottweiler amongst poodles and he volunteered to act as security.

Suddenly Cuthbert was re-christened 'Able', Percy was 'Baker' and Ronald was 'Charlie.' The walk had become 'The operation', the destination had become 'Designated target area' and all conversations were to be addressed to Roger.

Cuthbert and Percy gave a co-ordinated sigh. From experience they knew that Cuthbert alone meant failure; add Percy to the mix and it resulted in utter confusion; putting Ronald into the pot as well meant they may as well stay at home.

Cuthbert had always wanted to begin a diary entry, "It was a dark and stormy night ..." but it was actually quite mild out.

Percy had found an extremely long scarf from somewhere, and by the time he had wrapped all the excess around him and tucked the ends into various recesses, he looked like the 'Michelin Man'.

They both stood in the farmyard waiting for Ronald. Percy was shining his torch up his nostrils to make his nose shine red when two disembodied eyes appeared over his shoulder.

The eyes were surrounded by white circles. It was Ronald in a black ski-mask with holes for the eyes and mouth. Ronald thought he looked like an assassin.

Cuthbert thought he looked like a photographic negative of a panda.

They set off to follow 'The old logging trail' up the hill and into the tree-line. "Quiet" whispered Ronald. "We don't want them to know we're coming."

"But they invited us," commented Cuthbert.

The trees closed around them and the path narrowed. The wind whispered eerily above and around them. Conversation seemed like a good idea.

"When was this known as a logging trail?" asked Ronald, nervously forgetting the need for stealth.

Cuthbert replied, "Oh, it never really reached that status. Old Mr. Biggle came up here when he needed wood to make a shed."

Ronald didn't pursue the matter. It was very easy to doubt one's sanity after a conversation with these two. In fact it was a black mark for sanity just being with them.

Percy piped up. "We had a lumberjack in the family." The wind eased for a moment as even nature took a breath. "They called him Grizzly Plumm."

Ronald stumbled over a tree root as he said, "Grizzly Plumm sounds like a supermarket reject. What was his wife's name, Victoria?"

Percy was unfazed. Story-teller mode had an inbuilt selective deafness. "Crossed the Atlantic he did, worked in the Rocky Mountains. Giant of a man he was. They left all the giant redwoods for him, one man and his axe. He used to say that it was just him and his axe against the whole of nature."

The walk continued as a steady plod through pine needles until the lack of sounds caused Cuthbert to ask, "What happened, then, Percy?"

Percy even managed to shuffle as he walked before he continued. "Well, the usual strategy was to start in the clearing and work your way outwards, cutting the trees so that the men in the clearing could start building with the wood and everyone could work at once. Grizzly was fine with this at first, but as he did all the biggest trees and worked the fastest, he was exhausted at the end of the day and he had to walk all the way back again. By the time he got there, all the good food was gone and everyone had packed up, so he decided to reverse the procedure. He walked a good way out and started chopping his way back to the clearing."

The walk seemed effortless now as Ronald and Cuthbert waited for the inevitably twisted ending to the tale. "Well, get on with it," snarled Ronald.

"Well," said Percy, "by the time he was close to the clearing, the carpenters had filled the area with sheds, cabins, chairs, benches and beds, all ready to be loaded onto the wagons. Grizzly hammered away at the tree in front of him causing it to knock down several more. They all landed in the clearing squashing everybody's work."

Ronald sneered, "I suppose that they went bankrupt without him, then?"

Percy paused before adding, "Some did. The owner I. Kea invented flat-pack furniture and sacked all the carpenters. Ooh, is that a light up ahead?"

The little procession stopped. Ronald signalled that he would crawl forward to reconnoitre but as it was dark no-one saw him and Percy stepped on him.

Henry had been ready for bed for some time. Lately he and Margery never seemed to be ready at the same time. It was as if the golfing rivalry had entered the house.

Henry hitched up his nightshirt, sat on the edge of the bed and idly leafing through his wife's book, he suddenly stopped breathing.

There it was, the start of chapter twenty-three. "The two men who were vital to the success of the mission were lured into the woods to meet their fate. From this moment on, success was assured."

The book was still airborne as Henry raced through the bar, grabbing his mobile phone. Nightshirt flapping wildly, he dialled as he ran towards the woods. All the phones were switched off. Damn Ronald and his security measures.

The group of three crept towards a natural clearing. Ronald led the way. Cuthbert brought up the rear and Percy stayed in the middle and chewed his scarf. In the middle of the clearing sat a single figure inside a gossamer tent, lit by small candles in little round cups.

The effect was ethereal and downright spooky. 'Charlie' went tactical. He tapped 'Able' and 'Baker' on their shoulders and mimed a complicated series of hand movements before disappearing into the darkness.

Both Cuthbert and Percy were still wrestling with the first assault on their visual senses and didn't pay him any attention whatsoever. They moved slowly forward with trance-like steps.

Henry meanwhile was racing through the meadow, trying to dislodge whatever had flown up his night-shirt as he trod on its nest; he managed to part company with the creature and paused to re-orient himself.

Gasping for breath, he replayed the passage over in his mind. "The two men who were vital to the mission were lured into the woods." He started to run uphill towards the darker fringe of trees on the horizon.

He could hardly equate Cuthbert and Percy as being 'vital' but they would struggle without Ronald.

His brother could be a pain most of the time, but at least he could hit a ball. He ran on, oblivious to the warning sounds of his intuition.

Ronald was stealthily circling the clearing. The balaclava made little scratching sounds against his stubble.

He hadn't shaved because the enemy could smell aftershave for miles in the woods. The tactic was to stay as plain and natural smelling as possible.

'Percy should be pretty much invisible,' he thought with a grin as a huge hand clamped around his mouth. Something large and smelling of horses whipped his balaclava through one hundred and eighty degrees until his ears stuck out of the eye-holes and he couldn't see a thing.

The rasping sound of cheap adhesive tape came next and he felt pressure all around his lower face. He couldn't make a sound! The smell of horses receded and Ronald was left roosting in the fork of a tree.

In the clearing, the ethereal figure silently raised a hand and Cuthbert and Percy came to a halt. A tremulous, feminine voice issued from the tent, the speaker blurred by the layers of material. "Why do you seek my wisdom?" it asked.

Percy was delighted. He had always believed in the oracle and after a few false starts, this looked like the real thing.

"We seek the wisdom of the ancients," intoned Percy.

Personally, Cuthbert couldn't remember asking anyone for anything lately on the grounds that 'refusal may lead to bloodshed'.

Percy sat down cross-legged before the apparition and tugged at Cuthbert's leg to join him.

Cuthbert lowered himself slowly, looking around the clearing as he did so. Some of the shrubbery seemed blacker than it should be and Cuthbert was convinced that eyes were watching them.

Being naturally suspicious of women, he tried, "Was that a mouse?" and was rewarded with a shriek and a rustle from two places at once. That convinced him; the women had set a trap.

Quite flattering really, thought Cuthbert, going to all this trouble to eliminate the two best players. Two of those thoughts actually bothered him. One, they were hardly the two best players and two, the word 'eliminate' did not bode well.

The voice trilled, "You, the gardener. What is your question?" Percy nudged Cuthbert enthusiastically and whispered, "How did she know that, then, eh?"

Cuthbert replied sarcastically, "No idea, Perce. Where she would find a clue between the cap and the wellies I just can't imagine."

Percy was distracted. He shuffled and cast a bashful look towards the figure.

"Well?" prompted the voice, causing Cuthbert to wonder if there was an hourly rate.

Percy sat up straight. "Oracle," he began, "I come from a line of high achievers. Throughout history there has been a Plumm involved in all kinds of dramatic events. Tell me, will I ever make my ancestors proud?"

Cuthbert couldn't decide which one was the worst at stifling a fit of the giggles, him or the oracle.

The voice composed itself and replied, "Surely it is the tallest flower which catches the wind?"

Percy looked abashed and replied, "Ah well, that's the problem, you see. Not being very tall, I don't get the wind."

Cuthbert smirked and muttered, "Lucky you. I'm a martyr to it myself."

Percy nudged him ferociously and snarled, "Shut up, Cuthbert, this is the real thing. My destiny lies here."

Cuthbert snapped back, "She's not the only thing who is lying here, mate. Just because she's loitering within tent, doesn't mean she's real."

The voice calmly interrupted with, "Discordance interrupts the harmony of the oracle."

Cuthbert could have sworn that the shadowy figure sneaked a quick look at its watch. Cuthbert leaned over to Percy and whispered, "Do you remember the last time you thought you had found the oracle?"

81

Percy mumbled under his breath, "I was tricked."

Cuthbert whispered again. "This is a trick too. The women are hiding in the bushes. I think they mean to kidnap us."

Percy sat upright, the blood of his ancestors pulsing through his veins. This was it, the call of duty, fight or flight, the moment had come. "What shall we do?" he asked meekly.

Cuthbert was thinking fast, they needed a diversion.

Suddenly someone called out, "Oooer, girls, that's not one of us. What is it?"

Cuthbert and Percy stood and looked around. Racing through the woods was a long white flapping shirt and it was coming straight towards them!

Cuthbert switched on his mobile and speed-dialled Henry for help. This caused the 'Ride of the Valkyries' to blast out of the woods and various pieces of shrubbery to transform into shrieking females scattering to the winds.

Grabbing the end of Percy's scarf, Cuthbert pulled it after him as he made his escape. The result was that Percy spun around like a spinning top and careered into the tent. This caused the candles to ignite the material with a dramatic 'whoosh' which left Avril sitting there with wide eyes and singed hair.

Cuthbert ran like a man possessed, possessed, that is, with a desire to escape. He held on grimly to the end of Percy's scarf, and every time it went tight and Cuthbert heard a bang, he simply jerked it free and kept running.

Henry meanwhile stood doubled over in the clearing trying to catch his breath near what looked like the remains of a camp fire. The last thing he remembered was a dark presence near him and the smell of horse.

Cuthbert slumped on the floor gasping. The over-stretched scarf trailed out of the farmhouse door behind him and Percy was still at the end of it, out in the dark somewhere. Cuthbert found his breathing rhythm again and started hauling the scarf into the kitchen. Loop after loop was coiled in front of him before Percy stumbled in, giving two last thumps as he hit each side of the door frame.

Cuthbert relaxed; they had made it. He had absolutely no idea what had been going on or why anyone did what to whom, but the end of the story was they were safe and sound - or, in fact, unsound, if Percy's antics were anything to go by.

Percy stood, with one welly missing and even more dishevelled than usual, rocking from side to side. First pointing at one site of an injury and then at another, he alternated between pointing and shaking his fist at Cuthbert.

He was thankfully silent during this tirade as the final end to the scarf was tightly wound around his mouth and tucked into his top pocket. Then he noticed the missing welly and fainted in the corner near the cooking range.

The old range paused in its routine grumbling, and hissed a jet of steam at him, but then gave up and slumbered on.

Cuthbert went wearily up to bed. His father had always lectured him to, "Never go to sleep on a problem". Cuthbert had refined this to, "Always sleep through a problem." That way it was usually gone in the morning.

Chapter Thirty-One

Cuthbert awoke to a strange clicking sound. He went to the window and parted the thatch to see if he could identify the sound. It wasn't outside.

Dressing and entering the kitchen he was greeted by the sight of Percy cooking breakfast in his golfing shoes. The spikes were clicking on the flagstones like a dog's claws on a wooden floor. "Morning, Percy," tried Cuthbert.

"Huh!" replied the reluctant chef.

Cuthbert sighed. It was going to be one of those mornings.

Cuthbert glanced up as his plate crashed down in front of him. Percy was covered in lumps, bumps and bruises. "Every tree," he was mumbling, "every blessed tree!" before he clicked off to fetch his plate.

Cuthbert nudged his sausages with a fork. Everything seemed to be wearing a carbon overcoat. "Having trouble with the frying pan, are we? Is it only burning one side these days?" Cuthbert looked longingly at Percy's 'magazine-spread' fry-up.

Percy slowly munched away on a perfectly cooked sausage before he replied, "Every blooming tree you could find. Every one." He pointed his fork at Cuthbert accusingly and asked, "Where am I going to get hold of a single welly?" he demanded. "How many one-legged gardeners do you know, Cuthbert? What use would he be, eh, stamping about on a wooden leg?"

Cuthbert thought for a moment and replied, "Handy for dibbing, I suppose." With his breakfast already ruined, he felt there was not much left to lose.

Percy slowly cut up another perfect sausage and allowed the aroma to drift across the table before popping it into his mouth and smiling amidst the bumps.

"Oh good grief, Percy, we will look for your welly this morning. Who could possibly want it for anything?"

Percy ignored him and slowly and deliberately finished his breakfast.

The crow was warm. He was comfortable. He felt safe. The problem with being a single crow was that every night was a night on the tiles.

If you didn't have anyone to breed with there was no point building a nest, and anyway, the female always declared it 'so last year' and you had to build another one. He could actually be a trend-setter.

How many other single crows had a detached dwelling with views over the country? Any fool could follow the flock and build right up on the top branches where everyone could mind everyone else's business.

Plus, the females could see for miles up there; you were never out of sight. Eyes like blooming hawks, they had. The crow nestled down into his folded wings and slept, causing Percy's welly to vibrate with his gentle snores.

Cuthbert and Percy bickered all the way through the fields and all the way up into the woods.

Percy refused to accept that Cuthbert had saved him from being kidnapped or even a fate worse than death at the hands of the women. He insisted that he had been in control and was using the situation to his advantage.

Cuthbert was trying to pry out of him what precisely the advantage had been. They reached the clearing and looked around in silence. A dark circle on the grass marked the spot where the tent had stood, so they were in the right place.

"Any great ideas, then, Cuthbert?" snarled Percy.

Cuthbert smiled as he suggested, "We could always run back the way we came, bumping into every tree and checking around it."

Percy glared at him and prepared to wander off on his search. He had insisted on wearing one welly so that the pair could be re-united immediately. He wasn't in the best of moods, not after the field of cows they had just crossed, anyway. He shook his foot at the memory of it.

Cuthbert took out his phone, pressed the button for Percy's number and waited.

Percy petulantly threw a pebble into a bush and they both heard a loud buzzing sound coming from it. "My welly, the phone's still inside it," cried Percy, running across the clearing, arms outstretched, like Heathcliff running across the moor.

His head and shoulders disappeared into the bush and Cuthbert was treated to the sight of Percy's backside as he reached into the depths. The rustling stopped. The buzzing stopped. The screaming started. Percy shot out of the bush and re-crossed the clearing like Heathcliff re-crossing the moor pursued by millions of angry bees.

Cuthbert looked at his mobile phone as if it had personally arranged this and firmly closed the lid.

Percy was steeple-chasing through the woods and increasing his lead when a homecoming squadron spotted him and peeled-off out of the sun to hit him from the other direction.

A loud splash in the distance revealed Percy's whereabouts and his strategy, so Cuthbert wearily headed over to take the blame.

Cuthbert had seen travel brochures for most of the exotic places around the world and he knew what the figures around the Trevi fountain looked like.

A sodden Percy emerged from the water, looking like the version sold by all cheap garden centres everywhere. Water poured off him as he stood and blew a spout like a killer whale. At least the bumps and bruises didn't look so bad hidden amongst the bee stings.

The crow was also awoken by the splash and slithered upwards to poke his beak over the edge of his new pied à terre.

He gawped in amazement. It was them! Whenever the crow felt pain, feather deprivation or the loss of another faculty, those two were never far away.

It seemed that the little scruffy one was going through some sort of baptismal ritual. The crow fraternity particularly enjoyed the outdoor ones. A well-aimed dropping could test Christian belief beyond measure.

The crow eyed the other one. He was standing on the bank offering a hand to the newly anointed one and looked almost off-balance.

The crow rallied to the battle cry of his ancestors, "Never turn a wing from the everlasting conflict. Spread your wings and attack whilst your beak is firm," or, as it sounded to humans, "Caw!" Forgetting that it wasn't wise to open one's wings inside a welly, the crow attacked. The welly accompanied him.

Percy was incandescent with rage. He was shaking with the cold and his body could not cope with all these temperature changes and running water.

He glared at Cuthbert's outstretched hand and was about to tell him where to put it when he saw his faithful welly fly out of a bush and kick Cuthbert in the rump.

Cuthbert joined him in the water and emerged holding the missing welly. "Good news, Percy," he spluttered.

The two sat on the bank steaming gently in the sun. Cuthbert had tried Percy's phone and it had emitted a buzz followed by a bizz, and then just sat there feeling sorry for itself. Cuthbert's phone had fallen on dry land and he dialled Henry's number.

'Ride of the Valkyries' echoed through the woods once again and Cuthbert and Percy squelched away looking for it.

The crow had rolled away into the undergrowth and watched with glee as the two struggled out of the water.

When they had gone, he flew back to his cosy new home. It had gone! He looked everywhere. He tore the bush to shreds and then sat back exhausted. 'Typical' he thought. 'No sooner on the housing ladder and I'm gazumped!'

Cuthbert and Percy looked around nervously. They had found the phone under a tree. Nailed to the tree was Ronald's balaclava and Henry's nightshirt. Also nailed to the trunk was a note with torn perforated edges.

Cuthbert recognised it as from Avril's reporter's notebook. It read, 'Two local men held hostage. Will golf team have to concede defeat? Future looks grim for tournament.'

"Looks like Avril's style all right," mused Cuthbert.

Percy tried to scratch his head through his soggy hat and failed. "I'm wondering why they didn't take us," he said. "I am wondering where they are and I am wondering what we should do next." Percy looked directly at Cuthbert and asked, "What are you wondering Cuthbert?"

Cuthbert looked at the nightshirt and replied absently, "I'm wondering what Henry's wearing."

The two walked home in silence apart from the hydraulic noises coming from Percy's wellies with each step. Cuthbert was forgiven; as far as Percy was concerned, as long as they ended up as wet as each other, it was a draw.

Cuthbert didn't remind him about the bumps, bruises and bee stings. As they walked, Cuthbert wondered aloud, "Aren't the women taking this rather too seriously, Percy?"

Percy stopped in mid-squelch and wrung out the end of an unidentifiable piece of clothing from around his midriff. "I suppose so, but it's not as if any of us will be of any use to them, is it? Two smashed plates and that's the last time we wash up. One load of pink washing and we're sacked. I really don't see much of a threat." Another layer of clothing was wrung as he spoke.

"Perhaps that's it," mused Cuthbert. "If we don't behave, something horrible will happen to the hostages!"

Percy paused from his hand wringing and grinned," Oh dear, poor old Ronald."

The two enjoyed the moment, but then conceded that Henry was actually quite a nice chap. They completed the walk in silence, each deep in his own thoughts, or in Percy's case, deep in his own wellies. How on earth would he salvage his emergency chocolate from inside one of the toes? He was betting that it was all mixed up with his seed collection by now.

Henry and Ronald had found themselves in a small room.

A single light bulb hung from the ceiling and the wall with a door in it seemed to be made from planks.

Ronald had been waiting for Henry to wake up. They had no idea how long they had been there or why they had slept so well.

Ronald tried to cheer his brother up. "Don't worry, in my line of work this happens all the time. Someone will push a folded piece of paper through the cracks. It will say, 'Hang on, lads, you are making a sterling effort. It won't be long now,' and we will be rescued."

Henry looked at his brother, "Sterling effort?" he asked.

"Oh yes," he replied confidently, "that's how you know it's the SAS. They used to be at Stirling Lines, you know."

Henry sighed. "Yes, I know all that. I was a war correspondent, you know."

Ronald sulked as he muttered, "Only trying to keep your spirits up."

Henry relented and apologised. "Sorry, Ronnie. I know you mean well, but it's not the SAS we're relying on, it's Cuthbert and Percy."

Ronald slumped. "Oh, so it is!" But just as the reality was sinking in, he stared in amazement. A folded piece of paper was being pushed between the planks!

"Look," shouted Ronald excitedly, "I told you!" He grabbed the paper and unfolded it. Holding it up to the light he read out, "Would you please be quiet? We are trying to sleep."

Ronald crumpled the letter and spluttered, "Trying to sleep … trying to … Hang on, isn't that Margery's handwriting?"

Henry stirred uncomfortably and admitted, "Yes it is. Had you noticed that the clothing we found in here was a perfect fit?"

Ronald stared at his brother and started to hammer on the wall. "Margery, we know it's you. Let us out!" The room reverberated with a booming sound and the wooden wall lurched inward, dislodging dust from everywhere.

Ronald quickly sat down as Henry observed, "I think we can assume that Arkle is on guard duty with her."

Cuthbert paced up and down in his kitchen. It didn't help him to think, but it did help him to avoid the smell of Percy's wellies drying on top of the cooking range. A strange green miasma was drifting around at will and Cuthbert was trying to keep ahead of it.

Percy sat at the table staring at two toe-shaped lumps in front of him. He was trying to separate his seed collection from the melted chocolate and old caramel lumps in front of him.

Cuthbert stopped pacing and stared at him. "What on earth are you doing?" he asked.

Percy looked up and replied, "Preserving my inheritance." He looked back at his task and continued sorting through the mess.

"Inheritance?" barked Cuthbert. "You don't have anything. You have never had anything. You never will have anything. What inheritance?"

Percy paused and looked up again. He pushed his cap back on his head and began. "The trouble with you, Cuthbert, is that you don't have a career to fall back on."

Cuthbert paused and allowed the miasma to catch him with his mouth open. He coughed and sat down.

Percy continued. "If life in the Valley becomes too demanding for me …" Cuthbert coughed again. Percy glared but continued, "I have my profession as a gardener to fall back on. My extra ace in the hole is my seed collection. Some of the best gardens in the land would envy my seed collection and right at the end, I will leave them to the nation." He sat back smugly.

Cuthbert studied the pile of debris in front of Percy. "Is that an orange pip?" he asked.

Percy snapped, "Pips are seeds. That's a rare hybrid, that is."

Cuthbert challenged with, "It's out of our fruit bowl."

Percy sat up straight and defended himself. "There's a Latin term for you, mate," he said angrily.

Cuthbert smirked, "I'm betting there's one for you, too, mate"

Percy ignored him and continued. "'Non-Compost-Mentis'." He paused for effect. "That's Latin for someone who knows nothing at all about gardening. You should be privileged to share my experiences, mate."

Cuthbert coughed again. "No, thanks. It's bad enough having to share your wellies."

Henry sat in utter fascination. Ronald had 'gone tactical' again. He seemed to be dismantling his clothing to reveal a comprehensive survival kit.

His two shoe-laces had become a Garrotte. One of his buttons turned out to be a miniature compass. He produced a short knife from inside his shoe heel and the flap of his shirt was a map of Sierra-Leone.

One of his pockets contained plastic explosive disguised as jelly beans and the other had a selection of beads to impress the natives. Henry could only hope that they didn't get mixed up.

At that moment Ronald was screwing together lots of slim tubes, all retrieved from various seams in his coat; he then removed a contact lens from one eye and popped it onto the end of the tubes.

Grinning at Henry he announced, "Periscope," and slid it through the cracks in the wall.

Henry had never been clear about his brother's occupation. Somehow, whenever Henry was in a war zone, his brother was always there first, setting up camps in jungle clearings and training the locals to sink wells using rocket launchers.

This was some sort of window into his brother's soul and Henry would rather like to have closed it.

Ronald pulled the tubes back into the room and announced, "Just the two of them. It's time to go, bro'!" He then began to flatten several 'jellybeans' around the door lock, unthread a length of copper filament from the stitching on his sleeve and unscrew the light bulb.

Henry began to cringe in the corner.

Meanwhile Percy had had enough. Cuthbert's last crack about giving him a light bulb for his collection had been too much.

He grabbed his wellies from the top of the stove, jammed them on his feet, swept his collection into his hat and stamped away. He was stamping partly out of anger and partly to put out the flames trying to take hold inside his overheated wellies.

Henry winced as a sharp crack was heard and then a cloud of fumes filled the room.

The door swung partly open and Ronald started to shoulder charge what was left. Bursting through, he found that under cover of the smoke, the women had gone. They had also closed another door behind them.

Percy shambled across the kitchen. It had long been his habit to rise early since he read somewhere that 'A gardener should always be up in time to hear his plants growing'.

He always opened the door and took a breath of fresh morning air into his lungs while Cuthbert pottered with the kettle. This morning was no exception. Percy swung the door back on its hinges and was immediately assailed by bright flashes of light and people shouting at him.

Shutting the door again and blinded by the flashbulbs which had left dancing shapes on his retinas, he tried to focus on where he thought Cuthbert might be.

"It's for you," he said and sat heavily on the floor.

Cuthbert clucked like an overworked chicken and went to the door, scowling at Percy. The room suddenly filled with blue and white magnesium flares as Cuthbert experienced the power of the press.

Cuthbert was forced back into his own kitchen by a surge of reporters waving notebooks as if each book was a talisman to ward off the evil of truth.

Several of them fell over Percy until he clambered onto a chair and watched the sparkly bits dancing around his vision.

Cuthbert was trapped in a corner like an undertaker at bay and the room was filled with shouted questions.

Percy took control. Standing on his chair he yelled, "Quiet!", and as all faces turned to him he asked loudly, "Who's paying the most?" He was met with puzzled looks. He tried again. "Who's paying anything?" More puzzled looks. Percy sighed. "Any chance of a free pen?"

One of the reporters waved a pen in the air and Percy dismissed the rest by shouting to an imaginary attack dog apparently called 'Satan'.

The reporter sat with his back to the warm stove and flipped his notebook open.

Cuthbert was instantly mesmerised by the light catching the metal spiral and moved his head slowly as he tried to follow the shiny wire with his eyes. The reporter noted the head movement and decided to speak very slowly.

"Is it true that a spate of kidnappings is sweeping the Valley?" he began. "Have two leading members of the community disappeared recently?" he continued. "Is it related to the golf tournament that the local women have been forced to take part in?" The reporter then used his trademark interrogation technique. He raised one eyebrow to an incredible height and asked, "Are you willing to reveal all?"

Cuthbert looked at Percy in horror. Had he managed to sack all the others and only keep the reporter from 'Playboy'?

Percy was no use. He seemed to be holding a one man gurning competition and Cuthbert realised that he was in fact trying to emulate the reporter by raising one eyebrow. Unfortunately, between the explosion of hair and the cap, it was impossible to be sure.

The reporter heard a low rumble behind him and tensed. The rumble stopped and he relaxed. "Can you confirm any of these accusations?" he asked.

Cuthbert tried, "Well, I think it is yes, yes and pardon?"

"Pardon?" repeated the reporter

"Yes, pardon," confirmed Cuthbert. The questions had come far too fast for him and he wasn't even sure he had them in the right order.

The reporter tensed again as a low grumbling sound swept around him from behind. "Er, is your dog safe?" he asked nervously, pulling at his collar.

Cuthbert looked the man straight in the eye and said, "I've never had any trouble with him."

The man relaxed, but seemed to edge forward on his chair. "Look, my editor needs this story soon or we will miss the next edition. Is there a mystery here or not?"

Percy suddenly intoned, "There are many mysteries in the Valley of Shadows."

The reporter scribbled in his book and risked a glance at Percy. "So, are you all living in a state of fear?"

Percy replied in a monotone, "Some of us should be very afraid."

Behind the reporter, the oven door slowly opened and the man felt a hot breath on the back of his neck. He edged his chair forward and asked, "Is there anything behind me?"

Percy replied in a deep voice, "Oh yes!"

The reporter began to quake. He turned to Cuthbert. "Am I safe from Satan?"

Cuthbert regarded him keenly. "Well, my son," he began, noting the sweat running down the man's face, "I only deal with the bodies. The souls are in the hands of others." He leaned forward and stared into the man's eyes. "Some people even doubt that Satan exists!"

The reporter slowly closed his notebook. He placed it in his pocket in a purely reflex action. The heat from behind him was unbearable. He felt as if his brain was trying to turn and look for itself. He heard a pattering sound as ash fell from the open oven door.

Percy asked solemnly, "Doesn't the public have the right to know?"

The man turned and screamed. There was nothing there! His chair crashed against the cooking range, closing the oven door, and he fled.

Cuthbert poured another cup of tea for each of them and asked Percy, "What was all that about?"

Percy shrugged and checked the farmyard. Everyone had gone.

The reporters in the bar of the Mandrake Arms were having a field day. Apparently, the local women were being forced into a humiliating golf tournament against the men.

Some of their husbands were being held hostage and the women were at their wits' end. Empty tissue boxes were strewn around like cartridge cases after a battle and the women sobbed continuously.

Had there been a woman reporter present, she might have noticed that the women were still photo-perfect after all that heartbreak, but the only woman reporter in the Valley was Avril, and she was one of the team.

The reporters were suddenly sucked out of the room by the news that one of their colleagues had turned grey after a supernatural experience somewhere called 'The Valley of Shadows' and was now a gibbering wreck on his way to be debriefed in Fleet Street.

The women checked outside and started to clear up the debris. Whatever Cuthbert and Percy had said, it all seemed to be working to their benefit.

The next day found a newspaper nailed to Cuthbert's door.

Apparently a group of Warlocks were terrorising some Valley, kidnapping men and taking them hostage and forcing the women to humiliate themselves by dressing in ridiculous clothing and neglecting their housework to play a game.

The churches were up in arms - or should that be 'alms'?

Women's associations all over the country were pledging support and offers of help were pouring in.

Cuthbert shook his head and threw the paper onto the table in front of Percy. "Just goes to show you," he said, "there's always someone worse off than yourself."

Ronald was running out of jelly beans. They had blown three doors down and they had used so much filament disguised as thread that Ronald's clothes resembled a game where all the segments were draped over a paper doll.

94

The last door splintered and collapsed wearily onto the floor. The tinnitus was now threatening to become permanent and breathing smoke seemed more natural than breathing oxygen.

Ronald left the room with a forward roll which left more pieces of clothing behind and he beckoned to Henry to join him. It was no use shouting to each other at all.

They found themselves in the old barn on Cuthbert's farm. This was where the Valley used to stage all the Shakespearean plays before a stroke of luck gave them the new building.

As both smoke and hearing started to clear, Henry observed, "Huh, after all that, we could have gone through the trapdoor to the stage. I wondered why there were hinges on the ceiling."

Ronald's mouth gaped and moved, but no sound came out.

Henry wondered if his hearing was back after all.

Cuthbert was used to strange happenings connected to a knock at the door. Sometimes, it seemed like a door to a different dimension.

This time, it was an unshaven Henry and a barely dressed Ronald who staggered inside. They blurted out their story and Cuthbert relayed the tale of the reporter and showed them the newspaper.

All was revealed. Henry recognised these tactics as ways to stir up the media, but what was the point of creating all this animosity?

At that moment Percy returned from the village with tales of strange events. Apparently, all the women were wearing clothing with writing on it.

Percy quoted several foreign-sounding names and then told of the terrible mistake Belinda the barmaid had made. She was wearing an anagram which Percy was sure should get her arrested.

Henry sat up straight as realisation dawned. "That's it!" he cried. "Endorsements and product placements. They have drummed up all this interest to get sponsorship deals. They could make a mint from this competition."

Cuthbert and Percy did their 'Easter Island statues' imitation, until Henry explained that the women would be paid to wear a company's clothing on T.V. "Their logos will be seen all over the country," he stated.

Percy snorted, "That's Belinda definitely arrested then. What with the anagram and her logos, she's in real trouble. He glanced at Ronald's decimated clothing and added, "They'll be demanding a refund from you, mate."

There was a temporary lull in the chatter as three brains made a concerted effort to ignore Percy and the chatter resumed. Percy carefully examined his wellies, but any sign of a maker's name had long deserted that sinking ship.

The four men fell silent and Henry took a breath, swallowed his pride and asked, "Cuthbert, we obviously can't trust ourselves anywhere near the women. Is it alright if we stay with you for a bit?"

Cuthbert nodded dumbly. It wasn't as if he was short of rooms, but somehow he seemed to attract lodgers like a sheep attracts ticks.

The next morning Percy went to open the door. This time he wisely checked through the windows first.

He stared into the farmyard. Someone had erected a gallows and left a scarecrow hanging from it. When he opened the door, it had a pentagon scrawled on it in chalk.

Bundles of garlic had been left on the window sills and Cuthbert's best broomstick had been snapped in two.

"Publicity's working, I see," said Ronald from behind him. "We need to establish a perimeter before dark."

"Why, has the fence blown down?" asked Percy innocently.

Cuthbert had appeared and was filling the kettle, and Henry was coming down the stairs.

Ronald had patched what was left of his clothes together and he sat next to Percy and started explaining all the gimmicks he had carried hidden about his person.

Percy listened and addressed Cuthbert. "And you thought my seed collection was weird."

Cuthbert approached the table with the kettle and Henry said, "Thank you, Cuthbert. Can't start the day without my coffee."

Cuthbert stopped and Percy muttered, "I bet you can now, mate."

Henry sensed that all was not well. "Something wrong? We will get extra food in the village. We won't be a burden."

Cuthbert was still frozen in place and Percy was watching intently.

Henry took a guess. "That's not coffee, is it?"

96

Cuthbert shook his head slowly as if someone had announced his death. This would always worry him because as he was the undertaker there was no-one to bury him.

Percy decided to explain. "Bad associations, you see. The embalming fluid Cuthbert uses comes in round tins and is a brown colour. You have to mix it with hot water before it can be used. Had a few problems back in the past, we did."

Henry and Ronald exchanged glances, "Tea will be fine," they chorused.

Henry decided to compensate and jumped up to start searching through cupboards and drawers. "You sit down, Cuthbert. I will make breakfast." He only seemed to be able to find empty spaces, so he whispered to Percy, "Where are the eggs?"

Percy looked him in the eye and replied, "Under the chickens."

Henry tried, "Where's the bacon?"

Percy replied, "Out there in the mud."

Henry was exasperated. "Well, where is the toaster?"

The cooking range obligingly swung its door open and coughed smoke.

Ronald looked at his brother, "Welcome to life with Cuthbert and Percy," he said.

The brothers returned from a shopping trip late in the afternoon. They carried boxes of provisions.

The trip into the village had been quite nerve-wracking. The women had certainly succeeded in drumming up bad feelings amongst the natives.

Ronald had collected his spare combat overalls and various items of the 'dark arts' from his room.

The boxes had been stacked around the farmhouse and Ronald and Percy were seated together at the table deep in conversation. Ronald was showing Percy how bits of his kit were hidden inside his clothing and Percy was all ears.

'Oh good grief,' thought Cuthbert, 'they're bonding.'

As evening approached, Ronald and Percy set off to 'establish a perimeter' and Henry prepared the evening meal.

Cuthbert watched as Henry stood poised before the strangely compliant cooking range, all sizes of saucepans ready for action around him.

After a moment to prepare, he swung into action, arms flying, knives chopping and pans clanging. From behind, he looked like a man performing a three-armed duet on a Wurlitzer organ.

Cuthbert wandered upstairs as strangely aromatic cooking smells wafted around the house. He had been depressed since Henry asked him to help prepare the ingredients for the meal.

He could see the food, but getting it out of its packaging was another matter. One box held another box, then inside was a bag. This could not be opened until the contents were scalding hot and needed asbestos gloves. Any meat was wrapped in some sort of transparent membrane which defied all attempts to separate it from its jealously guarded contents.

At the end of it all Cuthbert's builder's bucket waste bin was overflowing and Cuthbert's fingers looked like a set of repaired inner tubes.

Gazing out of the upstairs window, Cuthbert could vaguely make out the figures of Ronald and Percy. He could tell them apart because one of them kept disappearing in a puff of smoke as he set his own trap off.

Percy wasn't too competent either. It was quite nice to have company, Cuthbert conceded, but somehow he felt redundant.

The women were delighted. The publicity had been brilliant. Companies from all over the place were sending them equipment and clothing.

The little touches of mischief around Cuthbert's place were paying off as well.

Margery was slightly guilty at her husband being caught up in it all but she knew all the right buttons to push when the time came. He would come round.

Percy, Cuthbert, Ronald and Henry sat back from the table. The meal was gone and the plates looked as if they had been washed already.

A satisfied haze hung around the room. Ronald congratulated his brother on the quality of the meal and assured everyone that they were as secure now as if they were at Windsor Castle, thanks to himself and Percy.

Cuthbert waited for someone to point out his achievements for the day but it was unlikely as he couldn't think of any himself. He opened the front door and stared. "Anyone order a burning cross?" he asked.

The Captain had decided to defect. He knew that his wife Elspeth had been sneaking out to play golf with the women and after reading the papers, he realised that it was all-out war.

He would be the fifth man for the men's golf team. He had written many letters to the 'Times' under his nom de plume of 'Disgruntled of the Valley' but now was the time for action!

He crossed the boundary of Cuthbert's farm by climbing the fence and started towards the hulking silhouette of the thatched farmhouse.

His ankle felt a faint tug and the night suddenly turned into a bright white light full of sparks and noise.

Old combat reactions snapped into place and he jinked from side to side as he ran. Hand on his helmet and gripping his rifle tightly, he headed for natural cover and signalled for his men to close up. Then the reality hit him; no men, no helmet and no rifle. What the blazes was going on? Speaking of blazes, why was there a cross burning in Cuthbert's front yard?

Ronald and Percy had burst through the door to confront whoever had fired the cross. Then the perimeter flare went off. This was an attack on two fronts!

Ronald signalled to Percy to arm himself and they headed towards the still smouldering flare. Ronald swept a fighting knife from inside his boot and Percy delved into his welly as he ran. The turnip fitted his hand perfectly and looked menacing in the moonlight.

The Captain was now faced with two shadowy assassins and a burning cross. The survival manual section of his brain was rather rusty, so he improvised. "Come on you reds!" he screamed, "Up and at 'em."

Ronald now assumed that a full assault team was racing towards him, so he reached for more weaponry. Pulling the wrong thing as he ran, caused his trousers to fall down and he tripped, then skidded and was firmly wedged under the fence.

Percy changed direction in sheer panic and fell over the horse trough.

The Captain burst in through Cuthbert's front door and stood gasping for breath. "It's Rorke's Drift all over again," he gasped. Then standing to attention he announced, "Reporting for duty! I, sir, am the fifth man."

Cuthbert was about to reply when the two defenders of the 'mission station' also burst into the kitchen, gasping. The two leant against each other for support as Ronald blurted, "Security has been breached, Cuthbert. Oh, hello, Captain. You can help us to find the intruder."

Cuthbert took in the scene. The Captain stood rigidly to attention, Ronald had his trousers around his ankles and Percy seemed to have a turnip up his nose. He pressed his lips together, turned away and put the kettle on.

The two women, Margery and Avril, gaped at the scene from across the farmyard. After exchanging looks of sheer disbelief, Margery said, "They really don't need any help from us at all, do they?"

The cross collapsed with a final plume of smoke adding an exclamation mark to the evening.

Cuthbert had lost all control over the kitchen. He didn't recognise the smells, the names, or the packaging of anything that was being prepared.

Percy was valiantly chewing on something called a 'croissant' and getting nowhere until Ronald took it off him and removed the cellophane.

The traitorous cooking range sat smugly against the wall humming to itself as Henry conducted a culinary symphony around it.

Even the Captain was involved. He had taken control of a diabolical looking coffee maker. It was all chrome and knobs and it bubbled away to itself before suddenly making a noise like a concrete mixer and producing a tiny cup of sludge. Percy thought it was a sauce and poured it over his croissant.

Ronald was not in a good mood at all. He had taken the Captain and Percy to inspect the perimeter early this morning and had found the farm gate to be besieged by, as he put it, 'pitchfork-wielding villagers.'

Spotting Constable Beeching among them, he had gone over to 'confer with the rest of the security element' and been pelted by potatoes. He was even convinced that the constable had joined in.

As everyone selected breakfast from a buffet, Henry suggested that it was time to face the media. "There is no surer way to rile reporters than to ignore them," he stated. "We should call a press conference and allow Ronald to allay any unfounded rumours about the competition."

Ronald's fork paused halfway to his mouth, but his brother had anticipated resistance. "We could invite that nice Avril to interview you right here in comfort." He added smoothly, "I think she rather likes you, Ronald."

Ronald was momentarily flustered. He had noticed her and was convinced that she had smiled at him once or twice. He nodded, throwing in a shrug of the shoulders to make sure they all knew it was really for their benefit and of no interest to him.

Ronald had led an extremely busy and complicated life. Romance didn't really fit into it very easily. There was that girl in Colombia who had blown herself up unpacking his suitcase without the release code.

There was the female assistant who had asked, "Ooh, is this real?" just before a loud bang in the next room.

He would never forget the one who was to accompany him on a parachute drop to rescue a kidnapped movie-star. She had packed so many cosmetics into her pack that when the parachute opened, it showered the jungle below with multi-coloured creations from all the leading perfumiers in the land. She disappeared completely and sometime later a lost tribe was discovered and praised for their 'vibrant use of body paints'. The perfumed cloud had spread out and destroyed the jungle canopy overnight, thus revealing the lost tribe.

Chewing thoughtfully, he considered that, yes, perhaps it was time to settle down. Perhaps he should use Avril to help write his memoirs.

He hadn't signed any confidentiality agreements because, basically, half the time even he didn't know who he was working for.

Percy was sent to the barricades to present a letter requesting the presence of Avril for a meeting. Apparently, he was met with a barrage of name-calling

"Satanist!"

"Devil worshipper!"

...and...

"Scruffy little Herbert!" ... amongst the repeatable ones. He was also subjected to finger-signs, for some of which he could only assume some people had forgotten to add the cross-bar to the cross.

Avril arrived in the afternoon. Her reply had been delivered wrapped around a brick.

As the protesters weren't exactly macho types, it had to be thrown several times in relays before it reached the farmhouse and anyone saw it. The only stipulation had been that she would not be left alone with 'that Cuthbert'.

When her battered old Land Rover parked outside, Percy was given the job of inspecting underneath it with a mirror. Using his new training techniques passed on by Ronald, he pulled out the telescopic handle and walked around looking under the chassis. Unfortunately, every time the mirror came back out and showed his reflection, he jumped, frightening everyone to death.

Cuthbert had been told to be extra-nice to Avril and, if possible, not say a word. He sat at the head of the table and adopted a pious expression which encouraged Avril to sit as far away as possible too.

The meeting began and was fine until Avril opened her notebook and Cuthbert's expression glazed over and he stared somewhere near her midriff, eyes rolling slightly.

"Look, he's doing it again," she shrieked, pointing at an oblivious Cuthbert.

Henry took in the situation and asked, "Do you have a spare notebook by any chance?"

Avril handed one over without taking her eyes off Cuthbert.

Henry placed the notebook next to Avril's and laid his hand over the spiral on her first book.

He then slowly moved the new book across the table until it was in front of Ronald instead.

Everyone watched in fascination as Cuthbert's glazed expression followed the new book, his eyes rolling slightly as he traced the shiny spiral from one end to the other and then back again.

"There," said Henry, "just an innocent mistake."

Avril watched Cuthbert closely before saying, "Oh!" in a slightly disappointed tone. But she fastened her top button up anyway, much to Ronald's annoyance.

The meeting went well. Avril heard everyone's comments and faithfully wrote them into her notebook.

As the meeting came to an end, Percy went outside and prepared for her to leave. This involved watching the approach roads and checking for suspicious mole hills where mines could be concealed.

He also approached the crowd at the gate to gauge the mood.

When Ronald escorted Avril outside, he rode down to the gate with her to reassure the crowd that she was safe.

They were quite relaxed in each other's company and Ronald was on the point of asking her out when Avril shrieked, "What on earth is he doing?"

Percy was stood facing the crowd at the gate and from behind they could see that he was holding his coat as wide open as possible. The crowd was shouting and starting to hurl abuse and potatoes again.

Ronald leapt from the Land Rover, and grabbing Percy, he turned him away from the crowd.

Percy grinned at him. He was wearing a tee-shirt bearing the home-made legend, 'Satanists do it by candlelight'.

Ronald dragged him away reluctantly as Avril drove into the crowd to a hero's welcome.

Back in the farmhouse kitchen, Henry was pleased with the interview.

"Gentlemen," he said with a reluctant nod to Percy, "we have managed to clear everything up. The press can now be manipulated in the usual way - a crate of whiskey and free cigarettes. Now let's concentrate on the game ahead."

The team assembled its equipment and spread out around the farm to practise any shortcomings. In the case of Cuthbert and Percy, this meant remembering how to play the game in the first place.

After a few hours of practice, Ronald had allowed the barracking from the gate to get under his skin and he started firing remarkably accurate salvoes at the throng by the gate.

The rest of the group gathered around him and watched in awe. Every shot resulted in a yelp from the crowd.

Not even Henry could equal this. Stooping to pick up one of the balls, he noticed a black spot on the surface of the ball. "Where did you get these balls, Ronald?"

Ronald completed his swing and waited for the howl of anguish from the gate before he replied. "Jasper brought me a box-full from the twins. I thought I would use them for practice."

Henry handed each of his team one of the balls and instructed them to synchronise their swings.

Percy and Cuthbert gaped. "Hit them all at the same time," sighed Henry.

The team lined up. The team swung. The team connected. The balls flew. The five white streaks flew in formation like the red arrows display team. The result was an impressive "Ow!Ow! Ow! Ow! Ow!" all from the same man.

The team stood with clubs resting on their shoulders as Henry asked casually, "Where is Jasper?"

Percy replied, "Poor lad's been grounded. Some nonsense about stealing golf balls and drilling holes in them."

The team exchanged glances and Henry said, "We need that lad with us as soon as possible. Meanwhile, we must retrieve those golf balls."

The crowd at the gate were well organised. They were old hands at this and they had established a tented village. Some were veterans of the campaign when they protested about the big American airbase being full of Americans.

Surrounding a bunch of Satanists was a bit different, though. Throwing potatoes was great fun, although it hardly seemed fair when missiles came back at them.

Most of them were grouped around one poor individual who had bumps all over his head. He was fast losing count and consciousness.

The sight of five angry and determined Satanists charging through the tent lines, screaming and swinging golf clubs sent them all storming in the opposite direction, leaving 'Bumpy' to pass out in peace.

When they returned one by one later, the tents were flattened, 'Bumpy' had an 'M' for morphine drawn on his forehead and all the missiles had mysteriously disappeared.

With the precious golf balls recovered, the next step was to free Jasper from his captivity. With all the crowds of protesters and controversy, it would have to a clandestine operation.

Ronald took over. "Each of you has been issued with a set of tactical overalls. Percy can tell you about some of the special features built into them. We will be the only ones in the village dressed in black and wearing balaclavas, so recognising each other shouldn't be a problem."

The Captain raised a hand in embarrassment and spoke when Ronald nodded in his direction. "Er, Elspeth and I have been known to indulge in a 'fun night' occasionally, you know." He lowered his hand slowly as everyone stared, but was really watching an image in their mind's eye.

Ronald shook himself. "Good Lord, man! Do you actually dress in balaclavas?"

The Captain answered defensively, "Sometimes, not always."

Henry intercepted with, "It shouldn't be a problem tonight because you are here. She doesn't go out on her own dressed like that, does she?"

The Captain replied in an affronted tone, "Good heavens, no," before adding, "She can't undo the buckles."

The team assembled outside and Ronald instructed everyone to turn their collars up. This revealed a red reflective triangle sewn onto the combat overall. "This allows you to follow the man in front," explained Ronald. "Every team member has one, the enemy doesn't. If we need to get out quickly, follow the man in front."

The team set off, bypassing the newly rebuilt camp at the gates and heading down towards the village. A yellow glow from the village showed that this was a rare occasion when the electricity supply was working.

On the one hand this meant that they would have to use the shadows all the time. On the other hand, all the young members of the village would be watching TV and the older ones would be inside afraid of radiation from the street lights.

The team jogged steadily along the back roads, little red triangles bobbing along in a line. Cuthbert at the back gasped to the red triangle in front, "You're doing well, Percy!"

The shape in front didn't slow down but asked, "How do you know it's me?"

Cuthbert took a deep breath and said hoarsely, "The cap and wellies gave it away."

The rest of the trip was completed in silence. On arrival in the village, Percy indicated the house due to be assaulted. They crept with their backs to the wall and Cuthbert found himself at one side of the front door with Ronald flattened at the other side.

Percy efficiently unfolded a telescopic assault ladder and prepared to storm whichever window the first team appeared at. The Captain and Henry covered the back of the house.

"Percy," hissed Ronald, "show Cuthbert how to operate the emergency signal on his suit in case we get into trouble."

Percy propped the ladder against the wall and sidled over to Ronald where Cuthbert could see him. "Right, Cuthbert," he whispered in his instructor's voice, "any trouble, just pull this and the team will know exactly where you are at all times." With this, he yanked hard on a strap fastened to Ronald's shoulder and caused him to disappear in a cloud of blue dye.

Cuthbert was impressed. "Wow, we will certainly know where Ronald is for a week or two," he said.

Percy slunk back to his ladder as Ronald frantically wiped his eyes. With a glare at Percy, he addressed Cuthbert. "This is a stun grenade. When I throw it inside, it will give off a flash and a bang. This will disorientate the occupants for long enough to carry out the mission. OK?"

Cuthbert opened the door carefully and Ronald threw the grenade. They ran into the house and made for the stairs as the flash illuminated the room. Cuthbert witnessed a frozen scene where an old couple stared at their new TV marvelling at the realism.

The attackers seemed to be in the room with them! Pounding up the stairs, Cuthbert followed the triangle on Ronald's suit.

They burst into the bedroom and Ronald grabbed a sleeping form, shouting, "This window, Percy," as he threw the child towards it.

Percy couldn't resist peeking into the lounge just as the grenade went off and all he could see now were large white flashes. He ran to set the ladder up at the window just as a child sailed out of the other one. Percy ran to the next window just as another form landed behind him.

Percy suspected that he was hallucinating; kids were falling all around him, all wrapped up in sleeping bags. They didn't even bounce. At a shout of, "Upstairs clear," the two men ran down and back outside.

Henry and the Captain came from the back shouting, "All secure," and the group stood panting as they surveyed the writhing pile of maggots under each window.

Ronald unzipped a maggot and asked, "Who are you?"

"Charlie," he replied.

Ronald continued, "How many of you are there?"

Charlie replied, "Twelve, it's a sleepover."

The team were dumbfounded until a voice came from next door. "Gee, if I wasn't grounded I would have come with you on that one," said Jasper with envy dripping from his voice.

"Get down here," snapped Ronald, "it's you we're looking for."

Jasper slid down the newly placed ladder and joined them. Lights were coming on all over the village until someone put a kettle on and overloaded the circuit. The houses were plunged into darkness and people were appearing everywhere.

"Make a break for it," shouted Ronald. "Follow the man in front."

Cuthbert looked around quickly and saw a red triangle moving away from him, so he ran after it.

Removing his balaclava to help his breathing, Cuthbert caught up with the red triangle and grabbed someone's shoulder. "Caught you at last," he gasped.

Avril screamed as she recognised him and was still screaming when she pushed him away and fled inside her house.

Cuthbert looked around, thoroughly puzzled. He had followed the reflector on the back of Avril's Land Rover.

Back in the village, a child was heard to say, "Wow, thanks, Charlie. Cool sleep-over!"

The team eventually all collected back at the farm. Jasper was allocated a room and went to bed.

The rest slumped around the table, exhausted.

Ronald spent two hours getting clean with special dye removing wipes and they all wandered off upstairs.

The next morning around the table wasn't quite the celebration they had expected. The door had five newspapers nailed to it.

Each one had a nail through the face of a different team member. The headline screamed, 'Local lady reporter narrowly escapes being sacrificed by Satanists,' followed by a lurid account of Avril's supposed ordeal at the hands of the fiends.

A special edition was nailed to the door at midday. 'Veteran protesters attacked in their peace camp by man-eating Satanists. Fired upon by devilish devices which disappeared before our eyes.'

The next morning's edition reported an attempt by Satanists to 'Abduct all the local children for their own devilish needs.'

Cuthbert observed, "Well, thank goodness the press is on our side."

All six of them sat around the table. Screwed up newspapers seemed to be everywhere. Only Jasper and Percy were occupied. They sat opposite each other, both swinging their legs under the table.

By unspoken agreement, they were trying to synchronise the swings so that they didn't kick each other.

The kitchen door leant inwards and Cuthbert recognised the wheezing sound. "Come in, Constable Beeching," he called.

The door opened, but the room stayed dark. Constable Beeching began his vertical limbo technique to gain entrance and paused just inside the threshold. "Morning, Cuthbert," he panted. Then remembering his inclusivity lectures, he nodded around the table and added, "…and fellow Satanists."

This was acknowledged around the table with depressed nodding and limp hand movements.

The Constable assumed that these were secret signs and continued, "Me and Constable Jellicoe have been sent to investigate rumours of abduction and military excursions."

Ronald corrected him duly. "Incursions," he said.

The officer beamed triumphantly. "Hah! Thank you, sir. You fell for my first trap and you are under arrest for all the things in my notebook."

Both nature and Percy abhor a vacuum, so he eased apart the silence and said, "Couldn't have been him, Officer. He was with us all night."

The Constable looked stricken and Ronald looked at Percy admiringly. The Constable recovered his composure and said, "Anyway, that's as maybe anyhow, but me and Constable Jellicoe have a licence to search the house."

Someone wearily corrected him with, "Warrant, you fool."

As the officer grappled with the complexities of finding out who said it, Cuthbert asked, "Is that a sprig of parsley in your lapel?"

Constable Beeching glanced down and spluttered. "That's for the vampires, that is."

All around the table people became alert. Jasper slipped away, using the table legs as cover, and hid behind the newel post.

The questions began.

"What vampires?"

"I thought you said we were Satanists?"

...and... "Who the blazes is Constable Jellico?"

Constable Beeching flushed. "I am in control here," he roared in a commanding wheeze. Stepping slightly to one side, he added, "Firearms officer Jellico, forward!"

A shaft of light showed as the constable partly cleared the doorway, but soon vanished as another officer charged into the gap and promptly got stuck.

"Oops! Sorry, forgot to allow for the flak-vest," muttered Beeching, lumbering clear.

The new officer entered, both hands outstretched before him covering all the angles of the room with his pistol. He wore a baseball cap marked 'Police' and had a curly wire running out of one ear and into his collar.

He swept the room with his eyes and arms and barked "Kitchen, clear" into his collar. He then ran into the next room and proceeded to bump into things and shout "Clear!" all around the ground floor.

Constable Beeching wagged a finger at the fascinated spectators and said, "Now you know what serious policing is. We are adapting a policy of 'near- zero' tolerance."

Henry showed his curiosity, "Near-zero tolerance? How does that work, then?"

The Constable mentally re-wound the ear-bashing his inspector had given him last Friday and repeated the edited highlights. "On the basis that everyone does something crooked every day, we would have to arrest everybody, so we tolerate some people so as not to fill the jails."

"So you won't jail little old ladies, then?" asked Ronald.

"No," replied the constable firmly. He fielded every enquiry in a very professional manner.

"No children, then?" came a voice from behind the newel post.

"No."

"No women?" asked the Captain, just in case Elspeth had wandered outside looking for help with her buckles.

"No."

After several roles and genders had been explored, Ronald observed, "Well, that pretty much just leaves the guy in the striped jersey with the bag of swag, then."

Constable Beeching's eyes lit up. "Have you seen him?"

Ronald was just thinking of a reply when a shape ran upstairs. "What was that?" he asked. All eyes wandered vacantly until Percy asked, "What do you think you saw?"

The Constable scratched his chin and murmured suspiciously, "I thought I saw the missing boy we have been sent to look for."

A gasp went up around the table.

"Oh," said Percy, "you saw him, too?"

The Constable drew himself upright and bragged, "Of course I did. I'm a trained observer. What do you mean 'too'?"

Percy shook his head sadly. "The poor little blighter. Stuck on this earthly plane, he is, drawn to this old house due to a happy moment as a child." Percy waved a hand around the table. "That's why we assemble here to try to help these unfortunate souls. The non-intelligent, the narrow-minded out there call us Satanists."

Constable Beeching sat down heavily. "Go on, then, show me what you do."

Percy looked at Cuthbert sat at the head of the table, wondering why he was suddenly the focus of attention.

Henry quickly produced Avril's spare notebook and slid it in front of Cuthbert. Cuthbert's eyes obediently began to trace the shiny spiral. His eyes rolled slightly and his head began to follow them.

Constable Beeching sat transfixed as a figure of a boy appeared at the bend in the stairs. Dressed in Cuthbert's long night-shirt, Jasper looked as if he was floating over the steps and his hands were folded in prayer.

Constable Jellico finished clearing the ground floor and stood gaping beside Ronald, his pistol held pointing at the floor.

Percy began to speak. His tone was fixed, neutral. "Can we help you, spirit?"

The boy answered in a reedy voice, "No, there are those here who would harm me." With this he pointed at the armed officer.

Ronald reached across and pressed his finger tip against a button behind the gawping officer's trigger, causing the magazine of bullets to fall out onto the floor with a clatter.

The policeman leapt backwards, dropping his gun and backing up to the cooking range. His flak-jacket seemed to spontaneously combust and he let out a shriek which cut through all the chanting down by the farm gate.

As the Kevlar plates melted and dripped onto the back of his knees, the officer ran for it, trailing smoke, as he screamed through the tented village in terror.

The occupants cleared the decks and joined him. Back in the kitchen, Cuthbert was nearing the end of his solitary obsession He had almost reached the end of the spiral.

Percy asked the boy, "Can you go in peace, now that you are safe?"

The boy's voice seemed to waver and he replied, "Yes, yes, I can. Thank you for guiding me." With that, he began to glide backwards up the stairs and out of sight.

Constable Beeching stood, scooped up his colleague's weapon and the bullets, and said, "What a noble cause! I shall make sure that no-one disturbs you again. This will be our secret."

After squeezing out of the door, the officer looked back at Cuthbert who was smiling as he completed his task. "You should slap him to bring him out of his trance, you know," he said.

Percy was appalled. "Oh no," he said, "I could never strike a happy medium."

Chapter Thirty-Two

With the 'Peace Camp' dismantled and gone, the training could start properly.

Jasper had elements of the Valley Mafia stationed around Cuthbert's farm on lookout. The team of five gathered before Jasper and listened carefully.

Feeling unnerved by having adults who actually listened to him, Jasper began to explain. "The twins sent me a boxful of homing beacons and transmitters," he began. "We bury the transmitters where we want the ball to land.

The beacon in the ball contacts the transmitter and homes in on it so that every time we hit the ball, it already knows where it's going."

Everyone looked impressed, but the Captain barked, "Can't go digging up all the holes, you know. Someone will notice."

Henry agreed. "That's right, we can't, but what if we dig just off the green, say slightly uphill so that the ball always lands in the rough but rolls back nearer to the hole?" This met with the approval of all those who mattered.

Percy meanwhile had been holding a small beacon in one hand and a tiny transmitter in the other, and had been miming to Cuthbert how it all worked as if he was a complete idiot.

Jasper turned on the unit and Percy's hands slammed together, blackening his thumb nail. Sucking his thumb angrily, Percy opened his mouth to wipe the smirk off Cuthbert's face and swallowed the tiny beacon.

Jasper was saying that they still had enough units left to cover all the holes on the course, but the section on Cuthbert's farm would be down to skill alone.

Each member of the team was given a young assistant from the Valley Mafia and a trowel. They set off to start planting the devices.

Percy seemed to have developed the hiccups. By the time it was dark, all the devices were buried and the team met back in the farmyard.

Jasper dispersed the Valley Mafia, not because they should be in bed but because they were behind on the protection racket collections.

Ronald was the last one back. All the team sat around outside the farmhouse enjoying a warm evening and the sensation of a plot well plotted.

Ronald was strolling back with a club over his shoulder and tossing one of the doctored balls in his hand.

The Captain had checked through an ancient telescope and had seen him making his way back so no-one was worried.

Ronald had ended up with an odd ball. There was no corresponding transmitter. He threw the ball in front of him and tapped it forward, catching it up as he walked.

Squaring up to the ball, he sighted on the farmyard. It was an impossibly long shot, especially in the gathering dusk, but the ball was no real use without the missing transmitter, so he swung.

Chapter Thirty-Three

Cuthbert was filling everyone's mug with steaming tea. The coffee drinkers had got used to pouring it away and refilling from the shiny chromium percolator which seemed to giggle whenever Cuthbert approached it.

Percy raised his cup and toasted the success of the day. Raising his cup, he turned at the last second to face Jasper and a golf ball shattered his mug, leaving the Captain dripping as if he was melting.

"Damn it all, man!" exploded the Captain. "Pour it discreetly into the flower pot like the rest of us."

Percy hiccupped.

Everyone clustered around Ronald when he returned, demanding to know how far away he had been when he hit the ball.

The Captain had estimated the range with his experienced eye and Ronald confirmed it. "Even I can't hit a ball that far!" But he was shown the ball lying deep in the mud and the fragments of Percy's mug.

Everyone went inside and sat down. No-one noticed the ball wearily free itself from the mud to follow them and come to a halt against the step.

The discussion flew back and forth across the table. Percy was unnaturally quiet, softly hiccupping to himself. In the end, Ronald stood and walked behind Percy. "Well done, mate. You've helped me into the record books," and with that he slapped Percy on the back.

The transmitter popped out and skittered across the table. All eyes focused on it as if they were witnessing the birth of a new world. It seemed to be the moment for someone to say something profound.

"You Herbert!" shouted Ronald as everyone exchanged looks. Percy grinned sheepishly and remained silent. Henry looked thoughtful and nipped outside. The ball had moved.

He picked it up and stood behind Percy. In a very modern pastiche of the demonstration of Newton's theory of gravity, Henry dropped the ball on Percy's head. It bounced off and rolled towards the transmitter before veering off and rolling off the table and across the floor.

"U-oh!" said Jasper. All eyes swivelled to the unfortunate soul who seemed to have the answer. Jasper's eyes flickered wildly before his shoulders slumped and he said, "I think the battery has gone!"

The silence was broken by the Captain. "We must get more than one hit. We sent loads of balls at those blighters down by the gate."

Jasper shrugged, "That was the test area. We buried several and one of the lads tripped over his shoe lace, scattering some more."

Several sets of shoulders slumped in unison as if the marionette had downed strings and gone home.

Percy trudged away into the dark holding the transmitter, wellies thumping in time with his heartbeat.

"Why me?" he muttered. "Why do I always have to see if something will explode or test for a missing bridge in the dark?" This memory brought a smile to his face. He must tell the lads that one, he thought.

"Are you there yet?" called Ronald.

Percy was carrying someone else's phone with the cover open to provide a running commentary. "If many of those things are still live," he muttered "I'll be running all right." Stopping by the farm gate, he turned and called, "Right, fire away!" Then he hid behind the gate post.

Henry realised that they risked losing the odd ball but the theory had to be tested, so each of them swung as hard as they could in the general direction of the gate.

Percy heard a whistling sound and stayed low behind the stout old post. Whistle! Clunk! These sounds followed intermittently as balls fell all around him but none of them was even close.

He heard Henry say, "Come on, Cuthbert. Just belt it in the general direction." Percy stood. If Cuthbert was the last man, he was as safe as houses.

Percy stretched to ease the creaks of the day when a faint beeping in one ear seemed to be getting closer to the whistle in the other ear. Then the ground came up to meet him.

Percy came to, trying to focus on some sort of clock swimming before him.

Gradually he realised that it was the pressure gauge on the cooking range and the needle was almost in the red. He had seen that before, just before the door flew open and incinerated next door's cat. He shuffled away and winced at the pain behind his eyes.

Henry spotted him and said, "Ah, you're back. It seems that Jasper was right. We can only guarantee one hit for each ball before the battery goes, so it's one major shot at each hole. The rest is camouflage to fool the women."

Percy muttered, "Never did trust electric. Never there when you want it."

Ronald spoke. "He could be right, you know. How long will the batteries last buried in the ground?"

He turned to Percy who was struggling to his feet and patted him on the head. "Well done, mate!"

Percy fainted.

The meeting went into overdrive. The tournament needed to be played as soon as possible, but how to sting the women into a rushed decision?

Everyone shuddered as Ronald suggested threats. The Arkle factor was entered into the equation and the idea was dismissed out of hand.

Cuthbert became nervous when a group of people went silent. They usually ended up finding him a job. 'Quick, Cuthbert,' he thought, 'get them talking,' saying out loud, "They are rather fond of oracles, aren't they?"

Henry replied with, "They won't fall for that from us, surely. We would need a convincing tale, delivered by an unlikely source, one who wasn't perceived as a threat." He focused on the starfish shape of Percy flat out on the floor and muttered, "Ah, bless!"

Chapter Thirty-Four

Percy stumped into the village. His headache had gone but his sense of grievance was still well alight.

"Why me?" he muttered. "Why is it always me? Is it my fault that I have suave powers of persuasion?"

The bar of the Mandrake Arms was empty. After last night's efforts, the team was mostly asleep and the women had never quite mastered the art of sitting on a bar stool all day.

Margery appeared from behind the bar and suspiciously poured him a pint. Signalling to Geraldine in the other room to keep quiet, she served Percy and watched him go to sit alone in a corner.

He slumped in his chair as if all the cares in the world were jammed under his scruffy cap.

Margery had a quick word with Geraldine to come behind the bar as another pair of ears, and she made her way across the room, polishing things and rearranging them until, quite by chance, she was beside Percy. "Not often we see you alone, Percy," she said.

Percy lifted his head slightly in acknowledgement but remained silent.

Margery tried, "House full of strange men not suiting you, then?" She was actually missing Henry but daren't admit it. "You can tell me, you know. We hear everything in here don't we Geraldine?"

Geraldine tried to make a noise like a barmaid but stayed looking like a museum curator trying to look like a barmaid.

Margery sensed that something was being hidden, and having the nose of a St Bernard rescue dog, she would dig until she found it. Sitting down she reluctantly patted the back of Percy's hand and asked, "What is it, Percy?"

After a moment, Percy replied, slowly asking, "Have you heard of the black swan?"

Margery let go of his hand. "If that's that pub in the next valley you can drink up right now, right cow; she is - had all the crisps off the delivery van before it got here last week, she did."

A startled Percy desperately tried to stay in character as Margery ranted about some rival in the trade. "No, no," he said, stopping her before she could invade Poland, "it's an old Chinese legend." He looked across at Geraldine. "You must have come across it," he said. "It even appears on heraldic devices, shown with a broken chain around its neck."

Geraldine, like any academic, had created a persona which could not admit to a hole in her knowledge, so she replied, "Oh, that one. Yes, fascinating stuff," finding herself drawn across the room until she and Margery were sat across from Percy.

They both saw him shuffle to get comfortable but thought nothing of it. "It's like this," began Percy. "A thousand years ago, a Chinese mandarin had a flock of pure white swans.

They floated on a mirror glass lake all day and sometimes they took off as a flock, turning the sky into a white cloud of grace and beauty.

The sages of the day saw that when the flock was in residence, the whole country was in harmony and every venture succeeded and every decision was right.

"One day, the youngest son of the Mandarin saw something strange. The lake was no longer calm. The surface was rippling and slowly, very slowly, across its surface flew a black swan. It flew directly towards him, opened its beak and without a sound flew off to the East. Thinking that no one would believe him, the son stayed silent.

"The next day, the Mongol hordes came out of the mountains from the direction the swan had disappeared into and the land was ravaged and the people slain or taken as slaves. The young son was reduced to poverty and he wandered the land warning people about the black swan. A neighbouring province claimed to have seen and captured the swan but it broke the golden chain which held it and escaped. The next day, the Mongol hordes attacked that province too and it shared the fate of the previous one. The Chinese have dreaded the sight of the black swan ever since that day, and if it is seen, the whole country rushes to arms and prepares for war." Percy sat back and watched the two women.

Geraldine said, "Well, yes, most countries have legends like that. So what?"

The room was gradually filling up as the word spread, even Mrs Biggle left her Post Office to listen in.

118

Percy leaned forward and said quietly, "It's no legend. I have travelled through the Orient and I saw the way everyone watched the skies. When one of the other merchant ships claimed to have seen a 'strange black bird', the ship sailed and was never seen again."

Percy fixed Geraldine with an intense stare. "As you no doubt know, Peking was called the 'Forbidden City'. Every walkway was covered by tiled roofs. It wasn't that we foreigners were forbidden. The truth was it was forbidden to look at the sky. That way no one could ever see the black swan and the Emperor would be safe." Percy sat back.

Geraldine, the professional sceptic, asked, "And the point is?"

Percy smiled, the smile of the sphinx, the knowing smile of the 'Mona Lisa'. "This morning," he said deliberately, "I saw the black swan!"

The room was in an uproar. Geraldine was trying to keep order, but by admitting that perhaps, probably, maybe, she had heard the tale of the black swan, she could hardly laugh at the tale now. But what could it possibly have to do with them? "When was the last time anyone saw a Mongol horde in the Valley?" she asked.

"That's the point," cried Mrs. Biggle "you only see those beggars once when you've been de-flowered and I bet their cheques bounce too!"

Geraldine paused to try to readjust to being back in the Valley.

Margery took over. "From what I can make out, whoever sees the black swan, his lot will get all the bad luck after a few days. Well, none of us have seen it, have we?" She paused and studied all the shaking heads before her and continued, "I say we move this golf match forward and demand that it is played tomorrow!" Gradually, the shaking heads began to nod. "Thank the Lord for that," thought Margery. She really was missing Henry.

"Do you get many earthquakes in the Valley, Cuthbert?" asked the Captain. The farmhouse seemed to be shaking and a rumbling noise was definitely getting closer.

Cuthbert opened the door. The breath of Beelzebub hit him four square in the face and an enormous pair of teeth were champing at the bit inches in front of him.

119

The gigantic horse slewed around and Arkle shouted, "Golf match tomorrow morning, nine o'clock sharp! If you don't turn up, we win."

Cuthbert managed, "Did you get that great thing to jump the gate?"

"What gate?" shouted the rider as she thundered away.

Cuthbert closed the door behind him and faced the assembled golf team. "Gentlemen," he announced, "we no longer have a gate, but we do have a game of golf!"

Percy had never been so popular since that time when … He really must tell the lads that one too.

Jasper was watching Percy with something like hero-worship. "Did you really travel across the Orient?" he asked.

Percy set down his mug and shuffled in his chair. "That was my uncle. He was a seafaring man. He had a parrot, a right manky old thing with one eye. It sat on his shoulder and went everywhere with him." Percy paused and gazed around the room until his eyes alighted on a blue and white plate high up on Cuthbert's wall. "Pass me that plate, Jasper, and I'll tell you the story."

Jasper climbed up on a chair and handed the plate to Percy. The rest of the team had the chance to escape, but curiosity is a fickle friend and they all gradually edged closer to the short teller of tall stories.

Percy began his tale by pointing out the scene on the plate. His stubby finger traced the river and showed where the bridge crossed over to the small building on an island. "That there is a pagoda. It must be oriental for pigeon loft because that's where the Emperor kept a magnificent dove. The breeding line of this dove went back centuries and was so valuable that wars had been averted just by allowing it to breed with a dove from a rival kingdom. The only person allowed near the dove was the Emperor's youngest daughter and she was charged with its well-being.

One day at the local market both the young daughter and my uncle met. He was obviously a bird lover because the proof was on his shoulder keeping an eye on him. They fell in love and quickly needed somewhere to meet in secret.

Foreigners were referred to as 'Gaijin' or 'White Devils' and so their romance was dangerous. The girl suggested that they meet in secret, in the pagoda on the island. No-one else was allowed there, it was perfect.

The arrangement worked well enough but during their secret trysts my uncle noticed that the parrot sometimes went missing. Having other things on his mind he didn't give it much thought.

One day they were interrupted by a serving girl.
She warned them that the Emperor was coming to find his daughter. Apparently another nation's prize dove had just hatched its egg and produced a right manky one-eyed dove and they were threatening war.

The young couple fled across the bridge and in doing so knocked over the dove's cage so that there were two sets of love birds that day."

Percy traced his finger over the plate.

Jasper was enthralled. "Who is the third person on the bridge?" he asked eagerly.

Percy paused and then replied, "That's the Emperor trying to give my uncle a bill for bird seed."

He took advantage of the moment and walked outside to stretch his legs. Most of the plan was in place. All he needed was a black swan. He stumped off down the track, "Now where is that flaming crow?" he muttered.

Chapter Thirty-Five

Cuthbert was having some sort of identity crisis.

The symptoms were difficult to recognise because he didn't actually have an identity.

People tended to associate him with either his trade (Oh, he's the undertaker), his lineage (Oh, you know, he's the son of the folk from the farm) or, if someone knew him really well, it would be, (Oh, that's just Cuthbert).

This morning should have been the start of a momentous team effort and in some ways it was. Everyone else was working just like a team but he didn't seem to be in it.

Henry was conducting the cooking range. The Captain had the percolator chugging away like a calliope. Jasper had cleaned everyone's clubs, except Percy's.

Percy was convinced that the dirt contributed to its character and refused to even wipe it. Ronald asked everyone to keep an eye on him in case he took the wok by mistake. Ronald had been up all night adapting features from his combat overalls into his golfing clothes.

Then there was Percy. Percy had been on cloud nine since last night. Anyone would have thought he had taken Troy single-handed, and now he had disappeared.

The crow had spent a strange night. His life seemed to be one long search for a bed.

He had tried rooftops but was sick of being swept off the ridge tiles and waking up stuck in the drainpipe when it rained. He tried the old bell tower one night and still had tinnitus from that, but last night though, he had been inspired.

He had noticed on one of his endless patrols that the scruffy one didn't go back to his shed any more. He had actually spread the tale that it had been demolished so that he could move in with Cuthbert.

The primitive lock proved no obstacle for the crow. After a lifetime of collisions and crash landings, the twists in his beak could pick anything. He had hopped into the dimly lit interior and looked around.

One wall was covered in shelves with shiny statues on it; he had attended a seminar once on a roof-top in Cambridge and learnt that humans had to celebrate any trifling success by having a little statue of them made.

Huh! If crows did anything as daft as that, making reproductions of them to sit around taking up space all day, they would end up with, well, a rookery, he supposed.

This thought led to an unbidden memory of a short-lived romance from the past. He had been young, impressionable, and let's face it, inexperienced.

Who would have thought that someone would take the trouble to make a wooden bird to keep the sparrows off his grass seed?

The crow found an area of bedding. It seemed to be a cross between a jumble sale and a rat's nest. He flapped and fluffed and turned in circles until it felt like home and then settled down.

'Not bad,' he thought. He had slept on worse at the Young Motherless Crow's Association during his 'Flap-year'.

Percy had stomped about the area for half the night. He had climbed up drainpipes, teetered about along ridge-lines, swarmed up a tower and hung from the bell like Quasimodo.

He was exhausted! Unlocking his shed, he returned to the place where he did all his best thinking.

After turning around in circles a few times, he settled down, and with a final shuffle, he wrapped a feather boa around his neck for warmth. Just as he was drifting off, he thought, 'Feather boa …?'

"Gotcha!" he cried.

Margery examined herself in the mirror. All the women had stayed together at the Mandrake Arms overnight and they would assemble, prepare and leave together, except Elspeth, the Captain's wife.

She had suddenly clicked her fingers in some sort of 'Eureka' moment and dashed off. Her traditional role had always been tea-maker, so she wouldn't be needed just yet.

Margery swivelled around and admired a husband's-eye view of herself, 'That'll do, girl,' she thought 'Welcome back, Henry.'

Margery joined the rest of the women in the bar. Belinda was arranging a bandolier of her favourite lipsticks.

Geraldine was packing a magnifying glass in case a dislodged divot revealed something interesting and Avril was sharpening her spikes. No-one else saw Cuthbert as a threat, but she wasn't fooled!

Belinda tossed her hair in exasperation. If she wore the lipstick bandolier across her chest, it hid her cleavage. In the end, she wore it around her waist like a utility belt.

Catching Geraldine watching her incredulously, she snapped, "What?"

The entrance of Arkle saved a situation from developing as Margery asked her, "Is everything all right, dear? I thought you were getting changed."

The mountain of tweed and sensible brogues frowned as two tables fled in opposite directions when she passed and replied, "I have!"

Margery inspected her troops. She swelled with pride. Equipment checked. Look-outs posted around the course. Media alerted.

She nodded at her team with satisfaction. They had the looks, they had the clubs and they certainly had the balls. "Let's go, girls," she said and led the way into a storm of flashbulbs and questions.

"All right, men," said Henry with authority. "Let's go!" He led them out to face a spotty teenager with a disposable camera who was covering for Avril. Cuthbert sensed his moment.

The others walked straight past the reporter who, when trying to lick the end of his pencil, managed to stick it up his nose.

"I am available for an interview," whispered Cuthbert. If he was quoted in the paper everyone would assume that he was in charge.

The reporter was taken by surprise. "Ooh, everything happens at once on this job, doesn't it?" He fumbled a scrap of paper out of one pocket and gripped the camera strap between his teeth.

Staring at Cuthbert intently he asked, "Phwat foo voofinnk fill?"

Cuthbert gently pulled the camera strap from between the reporter's teeth and asked, "Pardon?"

The lad recovered enough to ask, "Are you worried about the black swan?"

Cuthbert laughed out loud. "Not in the slightest!" He hadn't even realised that the pub in the next valley had entered a team, and so the two of them chatted away together weaving a web of confusion so thick that it could be used to raise the Titanic.

Halfway along the farm track, they were joined by Percy. He had his golf clubs sticking out of one welly and in the other one was a crow with an elastic band around its beak. No-one bothered to ask.

The women had posed in every combination possible and answered vital questions about fashion and the woman-honed killer instincts needed to win a game like this.

A cameraman standing on the horse trough for a better shot suddenly asked, "What the devil is that?"

The media crowd parted and everyone focused on a column of belching smoke approaching rapidly from behind the houses. Fires were not uncommon in the Valley but this was some barbecue!

The cameras clicked as Elspeth thundered into view behind the milkman's horse. She was sitting on a wagon carrying an enormous oven with its own chimney and collection of spatulas dangling from the sides.

Pulling up in a shower of sparks and the clatter of contradictory hoof beats, Elspeth shouted, "Found the Captain's old field kitchen. Thought I'd fire it up and use it today. Meet you there!"

With a wave and a flick of the wrist, they were off again, leaving the photographers wiping oily smoke deposits from their lenses.

When the noise allowed, Geraldine leaned over to Margery and whispered, "Can you imagine helping those two to move house?"

Margery raised two perfectly manicured eyebrows at the thought.

At last the Press were happy and the women walked around the corner into the car park. There, in a gleaming row, were the five new golf carts loaned by the sponsors for the occasion. They even had striped sun canopies.

The women checked that their clubs, bags and accessories were safely stowed and set off.

Margery led the way, trying to outrun a persistent woman with a clip-board. The woman was gasping, "Now don't forget, try to mention the sun cream. Always flick your hair back so the camera can see the name on the sunglasses, and accidentally drop the packet of canine tooth whitener as many times as you can."

Margery had her foot pressed right to the floor but couldn't shake her off until a slip of the wheel knocked her into a ditch.

The convoy was filmed all the way to the course where they were met by batteries of cameras and hordes of spectators. They dismounted and began to sign autographs.

Percy had left their tracked all-terrain golf cart parked on the main road after Cuthbert complained about his farm track being redistributed behind it everywhere it went. Percy stood and looked at it with pride; the rest looked at it in horror.

He had painted it a sickly fungal green and he hopped aboard as if he was about to occupy the next page after the Montgolfier brothers in the annals of achievement.

Ronald looked askance. "A green truck on a golf course. How will we find it?"

Percy answered by turning the key. All sensation between the ears and the brain ceased to function. It was a sound that could be felt but not heard.

Everyone clambered aboard and copied Henry who had taken the woolly covers off his clubs and stuffed them in his ears.

Percy set off. The machinery ground its teeth and screeched and crashed until he realised that he was changing gears with the golf club stuck in his welly.

The ride then settled into something akin to a roller skate derby down a corrugated Cresta run.

Sir Toby Topham was in place to adjudicate the competition. This was his retirement job and as such he took it far more seriously than anything he had ever been paid for.

Besides, that Margery was a damn fine gal! Looking up from his list of entrants and his stop-watch, he groaned. It looked like the council had sent a tractor to remove the caravans.

Probably thought it was a travellers' camp or something. He stood in the middle of the road and held up his hand.

Several events added to the sequence required for the conclusion of this gesture.

Percy saw him and threw his golf club into reverse. The tractor carried on. The crow jabbed its beak into his left leg. The tractor slewed left.

The crow then tried the right leg and the tractor slewed right, ripping up the cattle grid and folding it into an avant-garde 'solar system' underneath, both stopping the tractor and raising both tracks off the ground.

Percy grinned at Sir Toby who stood ashen-faced as one of the tracks went 'flub-flub-flub' against the edge of his clip-board.

"I don't think he likes us," noted Cuthbert as they lugged all their equipment over to the first tee.

Percy grumbled that the device should have been allowed because it was a 'track and field' event but brightened up when he saw five ice-cream carts ahead.

Mass depression returned when the women zoomed ahead and selected their clubs for the off.

Percy was temporarily revived by the smell of hot dogs and changed course like a hunting dog, only to come back dragging his tail when Elspeth waved a spatula at him.

The men stood and watched as the women teed-off. The chequered tweed stretched across Arkle's rump went from stretched to undulating in a second, like a computer simulation of the map of the earth.

The ball almost burst into flames. The clicking of camera shutters increased noticeably as either Margery or Belinda addressed the ball and the crowd seemed to follow the ball with a sigh as material stretched taut and the ball left the tee.

Avril and Geraldine became uncomfortably aware of their supporting role as interest declined when they had their turn.

The ladies stepped beneath a special parasol erected for them, emblazoned with, 'Can't mention your problem? We can,' for a product called 'Shush!'

The ladies watched, drinks in hand, as Henry sent a very good ball high and straight. Ronald followed with a similar solid starter. The Captain brought whoops of admiration at the force and trajectory he produced and was rewarded by a round of applause.

Percy approached the tee. Shoving the crow firmly down inside one welly, he removed a club from the other one.

Sir Toby Topham coughed indignantly and spluttered, "That's not a regulation portable contrivance for the purpose of transporting and distributing golf clubs, unquote!"

Henry leaned over and said quietly, "Do you really want to confiscate it and keep it safe?" The adjudicator reddened and waved the game on.

Percy stood, Percy wiggled, Percy swung and Percy sliced. The ball screamed off at an angle, climbing rapidly and causing the women to spill their drinks as it tore a hole through the huge parasol.

"That's a problem they can't mention," observed Cuthbert.

"Shush!" said Percy with a grin.

Cuthbert approached the tee. He had no idea how many points Percy had just cost them. He supposed that someone somewhere was keeping score.

Staring down at the ball, he judged his target distance, spread his feet, pretended he was in his back yard and swung.

The women giggled, the ball sailed past them and hit the hand-brake on Avril's cart. The cart began to roll. Several gallant chaps started to run after it but when Avril shouted, "That's my cart!" they lost interest and it went to explore the bottom of the lake.

Margery shook her head at Avril's mistake; feminine wiles just couldn't be passed on, she thought.

The crowd went wild. This was bringing golf into the world of entertainment where most suspected that it belonged.

Henry sidled up to Cuthbert and hissed, "Now that, my boy, is team-work. Well done."

The women drove away, with Avril grimly hanging on to the back of Arkle's cart. The vast majority of the crowd followed at a brisk pace.

The men cast envious glances at the retreating vehicles, and hefting their bags, started to follow. A rather strange assortment had stayed behind with the men. It seemed to be a convention representing woolly bobble-hats and loud umbrellas.

Progress halted at the sound of a scuffle from behind. Percy stood swinging his club above his head like Spartacus holding off the Roman army. The men dropped their bags and went back.

"What happened?" asked The Captain.

Percy spoke through gritted teeth. "They surrounded me and when I followed you, they came after me."

He was desperately shifting eye contact to keep them all in sight at once.

Henry reassured him sadly. "Yes, it's all normal, I'm afraid. The glamorous side of golf has followed the women. We are left with the aficionados."

Ronald gasped. "What's that, a mariachi band?"

Henry elaborated. "This is the hard core of the following elite. They will be able to describe every shot we make over lemonade at the pub tonight. They even award a prize based on merit."

Percy brightened up. "Oh!" he said.

Henry added, "It's a golden anorak."

"Oh!" said Percy.

They walked on. Percy kept checking behind him as the muttering and scratching of pencils followed them. "But they keep staring at me," he said to Henry.

Henry replied absently, "Yes, they do that."

Percy continued, "And they've got umbrellas."

"Always," replied Henry.

Percy tried again. "One of them keeps scratching."

Henry glanced back. "Better walk a bit faster, then, mate."

At last they arrived where most of the balls had landed. The crowd showed its displeasure at the wait by ignoring them.

The women gave them a second, just to be polite, and began to play. The men, who sat rasping and aching on the grass, could only judge by the thrilled noises that things were going very well for the favourites.

When the women and their fragrance had led the main crowd away, Henry found his ball. It was neatly pushed into the ground in the middle of the print from a very sensible brogue.

Accompanied by frantic writing, muttering and scratching from behind, he replaced the ball and drove off.

Ronald, a little further on, had found three little piles of dust. "I hope someone's counting Arkle's strokes," he said.

Percy was still unnerved by the aficionados watching his every move, and having the others twisting and turning him before he aimed-off wasn't helping.

Henry gathered everybody around him and announced, "From the next hole we have to start using the special balls. We have to get rid of this lot." He nodded towards the watching assortment of charity shop window dummies and Specsaver rejects.

Percy rummaged in his coat and said, "Leave it to me." He went just behind a nearby bush with only 'Scratchy' following him, and returned a little while later, alone but scratching his neck.

He positioned himself between his team and the small crowd, opened his coat wide and flashed them.

The crowd was stunned, then appalled, then interested, and then they ran away. Percy turned, grinning. He had a chunky felt tip between his teeth and his tee-shirt said …

REAL PLAYERS DO IT BEST ON THE LEVEL

Free tee-shirts at the entrance gate

"How did that work?" asked Cuthbert.

Percy closed his coat and said. "Well, looking at them, I thought they must be either golfers, Masons, or both!"

"And Scratchy?" asked Ronald.

Percy looked worried. "It's his tee-shirt," he said, scratching under one arm.

The women had completed another hole and some bright spark had started releasing balloons every time they had finished each hole.

The multi-coloured balloons were printed with logos and bumbled up into the sky in huge colourful clouds.

The ladies were all enjoying the attention; they could really get used to it.

The men waited patiently for the carnival to move on before they teed off this time.

Jasper answered the walkie-talkie and watched the hole.

Henry placed the ball with the black spot on the tee, shut his eyes theatrically and drove it in any old direction. And that's exactly where it went.

They didn't need Jasper to tell them it hadn't landed. It wasn't even on its way.

A muffled cry of "Oops!" turned all attention to Percy. He stood with the offending felt-tip in his hand and muttered, "I tested it on the ball before I wrote on the tee-shirt."

Henry was livid. The adjudicator would have been watching through binoculars and seen the foul stroke. Now, instead of moving ahead, they were further behind.

"Look on the bright side, brother," said Ronald. "He'll be dead one day," and he placed a ball with a black spot on his tee.

Henry glared at Percy and replied, "Yes, but with Cuthbert burying him what chance has he got of staying there?"

Ronald addressed the ball. "Right, you electronic homing ball, you know where to go," and with that, he swung. The ball arced upwards, describing the ideal rate of climb, and went straight for the distant green.

The walkie-talkie chirruped, "Hole in one," shouted Jasper. The men cheered and they slapped each other on the back, a bit too hard for Percy's taste.

After hugging Cuthbert for the second time, Percy asked, "Have we won?"

Cuthbert looked around. "No idea. I thought it was some sort of ritual."

They trudged after the others.

The group around the women was in a sombre mood.

Henry didn't help when he loudly complained, "Oh look, chaps, we have missed the balloons. I hope they haven't run out."

The seed of doubt was planted in the sediment of suspicion and the women exchanged glances.

Margery mounted her cart, raised her club to the sky and shrieked, "Ladies, let the games begin," and ran over Henry's foot.

The crowd was energised. Score-cards were left behind - some things just didn't have their own column.

Cuthbert managed to bend Arkle's steering column with a well-aimed shot, leaving her and Avril going round in circles like two truants on an infant school playground.

Another cart ground to a halt after Percy stood behind it for a few moments. Apparently, the battery connections were wet.

Setting off for the next hole, the women clung to the remaining two carts like travellers on the Calcutta express.

The men managed another creditable hole-in-one to boost Henry's score back up to where it should have been, and on they went.

Arkle sidled up to Percy and put her weight behind pushing down on the club he kept in his boot. It took the whole team fifteen minutes to dig it and his welly out of the ground.

Avril stood beside the Captain and pretended to take a phone call from her editor about kinky goings on in the village and assured the imaginary caller that she would expose the man in the next edition.

Unfortunately for her, there is nothing kinky about a lot of buckles to the military man and he thought nothing of it. In fact, he holed in two as the talk of buckles honed his concentration.

Brenda seemed to be in the first stages of dropsy. Every time one of the men was about to shoot, she dropped something.

The revealed cleavage as she then picked the item up would have distracted a dead man. As it happened, she picked on Cuthbert who was the next best thing and it had no effect whatsoever.

Arkle had resorted to growling just as a man raised his club and somehow the golf cart carrying her always ran over the tee just before the men had a turn.

No balloons had been released for some time, but the two teenagers at the back kept on inflating them. After all, they were paid by the dozen.

The young lady wearing the sponsors' sash and holding the accumulated balloons was having trouble staying on the ground.

There seemed to have been a shift in popularity amongst the crowd. The traditional support of the 'little man' had come to the fore and quite a lot of people were now staying behind to watch the men.

Percy was just giving the crowd a speech to distract them when Henry contacted Jasper. The head of the Valley Mafia confirmed that all was well before hesitating and saying, "That's odd!"

Henry delayed his swing and asked, "What's odd, Jasper?"

Jasper replied, "I can smell horse!" The walkie-talkie went dead.

Henry made a tactical decision. If Jasper had been nobbled, he would just have time for one last hole-in-one.

He swung, and the crowd gasped at the precision of the ball's flight. Then they gasped as the ball changed direction in mid-flight and headed for the trees.

132

Henry busied himself with rearranging his clubs and walked away showing a nonchalance that he didn't feel.

He could see that Margery was standing very close to Sir Toby, and seeing him, waved and called gaily, "It seems that we are now equal, gentlemen. May the best woman win."

The women moved on and the men gathered for a conference. "We've lost Jasper and we can assume that the thoroughbred is removing the gizmos as we speak," said Henry. "Anyone with a dirty, underhand plan, now's the time to put it into action," he added.

The Captain broke the silence. "I blame those radio things myself. Never did get on with them. Old Blinky Blenkinsopp once sent us a message on one of those things. Distracted us at the wrong moment, I can tell you."

Ronald paid attention. "What happened?" he asked.

"Well," supplied the Captain, "he sent, 'Send reinforcements, we're going to advance.' But we thought he said, 'Send three and four pence we're going to a dance.' It was Blinky, after all."

Ronald steeled himself and asked, "And?"

The Captain replied, "Well, we were that busy scraping all our loose change together, we lost Singapore."

Ronald and Henry walked away together. Of all the things in the world they didn't need, it was another Percy. As if by some diabolical auto-suggestion, Percy ran past in front shouting "Leave this to me chaps."

Ronald turned to Henry. "Does that make you feel any better?"

Cuthbert, meanwhile, had been day-dreaming amongst the crowd when a young man handed him a bunch of balloons and asked if he would pass them to 'the young lady in the sash.'

Pushing through the crowd, he headed towards the gaily coloured orbs in front of him. Coming out of the crowd, he pressed the balloons into the young lady's hands and looked for his team.

Avril who had just agreed to be photographed in the sponsors' sash and holding the balloons, felt her feet leave the ground, and looking down saw Cuthbert hurrying away. "You," she screamed, "help, help, get me down!"

Percy frowned as the scream broke his concentration. The women were teeing off and Margery was just about to swing.

Percy stayed in the long grass and removed the crow from inside of his welly.

The crow felt his head swim in the fresh air as Percy removed the rubber band and kicked him diagonally across the fairway.

The crow, light-headed and disorientated, tried slow, powerful flaps of his wings to gain height. Somewhere below, a woman screamed, "Arghhh! Look it's the black swan!"

The women looked. Sure enough, this big, black bird was beating its way across the sky above them just before it ran into a dazzling stack of multi-coloured balloons.

The crow shrieked as the flak burst all around him. His late uncle had been born on an R.A.F. station during the war and grew up thinking he was a Lancaster bomber. He had lost a few tail feathers over Berlin and had described it when he got home.

Avril shrieked as the balloons burst all around her and she started to fall. Geraldine shrieked as she saw Avril heading towards the cart she was sitting in and Cuthbert shrieked because everyone else was shrieking.

Avril crashed through the canopy just as Geraldine jumped out. The canopy saved Avril but the suspension was wrecked.

One cart left!

The women fussed around Avril and Geraldine, standing them up, patting them down and doing complicated things with bra-straps.

Margery suddenly glanced around and asked, "Are you all right, dear?"

Arkle had removed her tweed jacket, rolled up her sleeves and was tying her tie around her head to act as a sweat-band. Next, she stooped down to the broken cart and wiped her hand in some grease. Applying this to her face, she made a pattern of two finger-stripes down each cheek and a hand print to her forehead.

Adopting the battle-hardened warrior's 'thousand yard stare' in the direction flown by the 'black swan', she muttered, "Get everyone to safety, Margery. I'll hold them off for as long as I can." With this, she snatched up two golf clubs, emitted a blood-curdling scream and charged towards the horizon.

"Where is she going?" asked Avril, rubbing her bruised bottom.

Margery sighed and answered, "To stop the Mongol hordes, I believe, dear."

Avril continued both rubbing and asking questions. "There was a puff of smoke from that hill top. Are the Apaches coming too?"

Margery concentrated for a moment before saying, "Oh that's Mrs. Biggle trying to phone us to say that Jasper has been sent to bed early. Poor lad hasn't eaten supper in months," she added.

Cuthbert was preparing to take a shot. Missing deliberately, he dislodged a huge chunk of grass. Geraldine sniggered delicately behind her hand.

"Careful, Cuthbert" said Henry. "You will hit the Roman layer!"

Geraldine stopped sniggering. "What on earth are you talking about? There isn't any sign of Roman occupation in the Valley."

Henry shrugged and remained silent. Cuthbert, however, was trying to fit the divot back in its place and was saying, "Well, you're the expert, but when Percy does his digging, he never goes too deep or he finds loads of these things. That's why we call it the Roman layer."

Geraldine sidled over, trying to suppress that terribly childish excitement which overwhelms the expert when confronted by lucky nincompoops.

"What have you got there, Cuthbert, dear?" she asked silkily. Her hand shot out with the speed of a striking viper and the silver coin changed hands in mid-air.

She gazed at it in awe as Cuthbert said, "Oh, you can have that one. There's another one in here." Bending down to the hole, he produced another coin, this time with a golden gleam.

Geraldine was on her hands and knees babbling incoherently. Then she stopped, stood fully upright and declared, "As the official semi-retired, stand-in curator, I claim this ground on behalf of the Museum Service. It shall be known henceforth as 'Geraldine's hoard'."

Henry nudged Cuthbert and whispered, "Typical, you wait all your life to see a good horde and two come along in the same day."

Henry turned away, as he was convinced that Geraldine was about to sing the national anthem, and saw Margery watching him with narrowed eyes.

He coughed politely and said, "Er, if your team would like to continue, we might just finish before dark."

Margery looked around. Geraldine was stealing people's jumpers, hammering golf clubs into the ground and then tying all the sleeves together to cordon off the hole.

Avril was rubbing her bottom and enjoying the attention she was getting at last and Arkle had become the Last of the Mohicans.

Belinda was … come to think of it, Belinda had never re-appeared from that bunker some time ago when a young man offered to help her find the ball.

Margery sighed and her shoulders slumped. She looked over at her husband and said resignedly, "Oh, all right, Henry, it looks as if your team is …"

Henry arched an eyebrow. "My team is what, my dear?" he asked, holding a hand to his ear dramatically.

Margery straightened her shoulders, "Missing!" she said.

Henry whipped around, scanning the anoraks, bobble-hats and vacant faces of those still following the proceedings. "What? Where? Who?"

Percy had stood watching Geraldine, jingling the spare coins in his pocket. Ronald had pinched enough from the museum to keep her peeling grass for days.

The only way he could be any happier at this moment was if he were taller. Looking down at the top of everyone's head gave him an insight into actually being normal size.

The cloud passing by under his feet worried him, though. Looking up, he saw a wonderful multi-coloured canopy of balloons seemingly tied to his belt.

Looking sideways, he saw a large black bird complete an Immelman turn and come streaking in to attack. Percy's little legs began to run and he drifted higher as his wellies flew off.

Cuthbert had watched Elspeth creep up behind Percy with a huge bunch of balloons. He had been about to shout a warning when Elspeth gave him a series of hand signals. She held one finger up to her lips, touched her chest, pointed at him and then drew a hand across her throat.

It took Cuthbert so long to work it out that Percy was already airborne and Avril was right behind him with an upturned golf bag.

Suddenly blacking-out was no stranger to Cuthbert but when the golf bag vibrated free and fell off, he found himself jammed through the canopy of the last golf cart, hurtling towards the ornamental lake, and all he could hear was Avril composing tomorrow's headline.

It seemed to be along the lines of, 'Local Undertaker undertakes to undergo survey of lake bed from underneath.'

Ronald had spotted the Captain doing press-ups on top of the field kitchen. When he wandered over, he discovered that someone had trapped his colleague's tie in the top door and the Captain was desperately trying to keep away from the heat.

Several really funny remarks instantly came to mind, but by then his sleeve was on fire, the flare in his top pocket was smouldering and his explosive shoulder pads were sweating. He needed the lake, so he raced after Cuthbert.

Sir Toby Topham fanned the score-cards out like a winning poker hand, studied them for a while, threatened them with his pencil, decided against it and bellowed, "I want all competing members right here in front of me, NOW!"

The Captain approached the spot with his tie still smoking and his face sooty, and took his place beside Henry like an embarrassed retriever.

The lake produced three dripping apparitions in the form of Cuthbert, Ronald and a sodden Percy, who had steered the rapidly deflating balloons towards a watery safety net.

Margery delegated several anoraks to guard the Roman layers fake site so that Geraldine could reluctantly rejoin them. Belinda appeared with a huge smile from behind a grassy knoll and Avril trotted up, licking her pencil furiously as she finished Cuthbert's obituary.

Arkle hadn't returned from her self-sacrificing defence of the unknown threat, but by the distant crashes and thuds, and the signs of trees bending, she was on her way.

Sir Toby surveyed the teams and announced, "Due to the absolute chaos in the fog of war and the miasma of smoking wellies, I have decided to call the result a draw so far."

The women exchanged puzzled looks but the men seemed positively buoyant, which was ironic as three of them had recently been under water.

"But we are at the end of the course," protested Margery.

Sir Toby adopted his best and most pompous tone, which he promptly regretted as he felt the breath of Arkle on his neck and smelled horse. "Er no, dear lady, the competition will now be decided over the extended course. Didn't you read the part about extensions, ladies?"

"I thought it meant hair extensions," said Avril.

"I thought it said we couldn't wear them," said Margery.

"I've already got them," giggled Belinda.

"How the blazes can you extend a hare?" demanded Arkle.

The men were delighted; the result was in the bag. "Meet you at Cuthbert's place, ladies. It's a long walk," shouted someone as they set off.

"They are up to something, girls," announced Margery through gritted teeth. "We need transport too. All the golf carts are wrecked."

Arkle raised her hand to her mouth and gave a piercing whistle which could have raised the dead and revealed a lot of Cuthbert's secrets.

The milkman's horse skidded to a halt, towing Elspeth's field kitchen in a flurry of dust and a clatter of ladles and accessories. "All aboard, ladies!" she called.

The men strolled along amicably to the rhythm of Percy's squelching wellies.

Valuable time had been lost looking for them, but Cuthbert knew that an Olympian sulk would have followed their loss and at least it stopped him grumbling.

Ronald was busying himself easing soggy pyrotechnics out of various hidden pockets and wringing them out as he walked.

This had caused him to drop slightly behind the others and so he was the first to feel the vibrations from the road. Next he heard a faint clinking and clanking and what seemed to be female whoops of joy.

He just had time to warn those in front before they were all swept aside by Elspeth's field kitchen roaring through their ranks, with the women hanging onto the sides, wildly swinging ladles and spatulas to clear the way. The huge food container lids on top leapt open as the rig became airborne on a large bump and the men were splattered with left-over soup.

"Argh, my eyes!" yelled Henry.

"Argh, my kitchen!" cried the Captain.

"Mm, chicken!" said Percy.

138

The women were grouped together in Cuthbert's farmyard when the men caught up with them.

"There must be some mistake ..." began Margery.

"No flags," said Avril.

"No holes," intoned Arkle suspiciously.

Percy bounded ahead and disappeared behind an old tractor chassis. Up popped his hat. "Here's one," he shouted. This was soon followed by, "Here's another one," and "Here's the next," until Arkle became annoyed with bobbing hats and irritating twerps and sent a ball screaming over his head to ventilate the barn the next time he appeared.

Margery and Avril had wandered into one of the out-buildings and discovered a long and well-scrubbed table.

"Is this ...?" asked Avril with eyes like Bambi.

"Yes, dear," replied Margery.

Avril slowly turned and saw the row of tall boxes and rolls of plastic tubing against the walls.

"Are those ...?" she gasped.

"Of course, dear," Margery frowned.

Avril then focused upon row after row of coloured bottles on the shelves.

"Is that ...?" she gasped

"Oh yes, dear, it's delicious!" enthused Margery.

Avril fainted just before Margery could add, "Cuthbert's Ginger Beer is renowned throughout the Valley."

Sir Toby had now arrived in his personal golf cart and surveyed the scene.

He could hardly back down and declare the ground unfit because he had re-drawn the boundary.

However, flustered by the protesting ladies and Belinda's cleavage, he allowed a compromise.

"The male team shall elect a representative to demonstrate the validity of this section of the course," he blustered. "Then a short break for refreshments before we end the match once and for all."

The men beamed and the women scowled with suspicion, especially when Cuthbert stepped forward. It was unheard of; Cuthbert only stepped forward to avoid a disaster behind him.

Sir Toby moved away amongst the debris and clutter of Cuthbert's outdoor filing system and called, "Play on."

Every move Cuthbert made seemed designed to aggravate the women: the careful positioning of the tee, the delicate touch as he placed the ball on top and the over-elaborate way he chipped it in the wrong direction.

The spontaneous and cynical applause stopped suddenly as the ball landed on the thatched roof, wobbled slightly as it followed the guttering, clattered into the down-pipe and exited into a dried-out muddy furrow and directly into the hole.

The women gaped. Every sense and instinct told them that they had been duped and the smirking clutch of men only confirmed it.

"Again," demanded Arkle.

Sir Toby was about to dismiss the request with a careless wave of his hand but Arkle still had her war paint on and a gleam in her eye.

The hand gesture turned into a wave in Cuthbert's direction urging another shot.

Cuthbert sighed theatrically and placed another ball. This time he even held up a finger to test the wind direction. The men stirred uneasily. They knew exactly which way the wind was blowing and he was pushing his luck.

The ball left the tee in a low, straight trajectory hitting a distant tree and disappearing behind the wooden barn where it clanged against a discarded plough blade, was re-directed by the hollow sound from an empty milk churn and reappeared bouncing along the top of the dry-stone wall. With a clunk on each step of the stile it came back to earth, trundling along the old tractor chassis and straight into the hole.

"Er, time for tea, I believe, Ladies and Gentlemen," declared Sir Toby.

The atmosphere around Cuthbert's table varied somewhere between strained and incredulous.

Elspeth appeared with hampers of food from the field kitchen parked outside and the kettle spat defiantly from the top of the range.

The men were failing to hide their glee by a very wide margin and the women were boiling faster than the kettle.

Percy had positioned himself near the door and he took the seat at the end where he could make sure that everyone was busy eating or drinking before he began.

Margery had suggested to him that Geraldine might be persuaded to pay for some of his remarkable finds out of museum funds. All he had to do was introduce the subject. He shuffled to get comfortable and began.

"Nice to see someone else interested in archaeology, Geraldine."

Geraldine's sandwich halted half way to her mouth. "Someone else?" she queried.

Percy leant his chair back against the door to stop anyone escaping and tucking his thumbs into his waistcoat pockets said, "Oh yes, my family have been involved right down the ages. We specialised in Roman remains. In fact my ancestor invented the Luigi board."

"You mean 'Ouija' board?" asked Avril with a snigger.

"No," snapped Percy sharply. "This was the 'Luigi' board. It only spoke to dead Italians."

"Did it work dear?" asked Margery condescendingly, deliberately encouraging him to attract attention away from a planned escape.

Percy took the bait and leaned forward in his chair, allowing Elspeth to slip out behind him.

Percy went into top gear. "My ancestors were able to interview Roman Centurions, Senators and even Caesar himself, but unfortunately it was the one with the stutter, and the pointer never stopped moving."

Geraldine simply could not help herself and began to ask questions as Margery knew she would. This gave Margery the chance to slip out.

Percy was in full flow now. "One of the best leads we had was after contacting a Senator who was buried along the Appian Way outside Rome. He described his vault and all the contents to the last detail. He even told us about a secret entrance. He said 'Look for the Golden Arches'."

"What happened, what happened?" squealed Geraldine. "What did you find?"

Percy slumped down in his chair. "We found the golden arches alright," he said mournfully. "They'd built a McDonald's on top of it."

Geraldine gargled as if she was drowning in fresh air and collapsed into her seat.

Henry shook his head in bewilderment and then stiffened. "Where's Elspeth?" he asked.

"Probably cleaning the mobile kitchen outside." The Captain waved a hand vaguely.

Henry looked around some more. "Where's Margery?"

Everyone looked around.

"Does it matter?" asked Cuthbert, lulled into a false sense of security as the hero of the hour.

"It does if they are moving things around out there," said the Captain.

Ronald laughed. "They can hardly move two tractors out of the way now, can they?"

"Argh! Where's Arkle?" yelled Henry.

Everyone collided in the doorway as Geraldine giggled behind them. "Women are like tea-bags, boys. No-one knows how strong they are until they're in hot water."

The men burst into Cuthbert's yard. There wasn't a piece of scrap in sight. In fact the whole area looked like a neglected snooker table made from dried mud.

The ladies brushed imaginary dust from their hands and Margery asked sweetly, "Shall we begin?"

Cuthbert felt the sweat break out on his forehead as he addressed the ball. He wished he could address it and put a stamp on it as well.

The pathetic clop sound his putter made simply attracted everyone's attention as the ball meandered in the vague direction of the hole and then began to roll back towards him.

Cuthbert's shoulders slumped and his self-esteem retreated to the dark place where it felt comfortable.

Arkle walked forward to inspect the hole, treading Cuthbert's ball right under the surface and leaving a beautiful smooth groove. Her shot was a hole in one.

Percy whipped his club out from his turned-down welly as he approached the tee like a gunslinger at the O.K. Corral.

The ladies were bunched together and really weren't paying attention, when even though he aimed for the hole, the ball whistled sideways and scattered them like pigeons in a cattery.

At the moment of maximum disruption, Ronald rolled another ball down Arkle's furrow and into the hole.

The men whooped for joy.

The women howled for blood.

"Where did that come from?" demanded Margery.

"Ricochet," said Percy smugly.

"There's no Rick O'Shea on the players' list," said Avril, checking her notebook.

The women glared at Sir Toby who could only splutter, "You saw the skill demonstrated earlier, ladies. Stranger things have happened."

"And things have happened to strangers," snarled Margery, causing the adjudicator to mop his brow and signal them all to play on again.

The atmosphere now resembled one of those foreign films where every face was shown in lingering close-up and every twitch was observed in detail.

The men watched the women, the women watched the men, the adjudicator watched the ball and the crow watched the lot of them.

He was actually wondering whether he could patent a game where the crows hit a ball from nest to nest and he could make his fortune selling worm-snacks and funny hats.

The last hole beckoned, but the men were starting to realise that the ill-feeling caused by either winning or losing would result in washing an awful lot of dishes over an awfully long period of time.

Ronald was the first to notice that most of the others were grouping together and muttering, and then Arkle turned to see what he was looking at and noticed it too.

"Is there something ...?" she rumbled.

Everybody automatically stepped back, leaving Margery in the forefront as spokesperson.

Glaring around at her fellow conspirators, she began, "Well, dear, it occurs to us that the original argument was between you and Ronald, and as there is only one hole left, perhaps you two should compete for it."

Arkle turned to Ronald, looked him up and down and sneered, "Sounds alright to me. What about you, Shorty?"

Ronald scanned the faces before him, carefully avoiding Arkle's. He surreptitiously tapped various hidden pockets to check how many flash-bangs, knuckle-dusters and pepper sprays had survived.

The result was none. Then he spotted Jasper signalling from the corner of the farmhouse. He quickly interpreted the nods, winks and wobbly hand movements as Jasper having hidden explosive resources in that spot for him.

He straightened manfully, adopted his best snake-eyes impression and replied, "Bring it on, 'She-who-blocks-out-the-light', and I'll show you how I dealt with the uprising on the Island of Poppadom."

The crowd gaped, Arkle was startled and even Percy was taken aback. He had often wondered where those thin, crispy pancakes came from.

As they all exchanged looks and placed bets, Ronald sidled over to Jasper and muttered from the corner of his mouth, "Well done, kid. What have you got for me?" Jasper looked puzzled. Ronald sighed. "I got your signal. Where's the stuff?"

"You mean, tell Cuthbert the kettle is on ready for when you finish?" asked Jasper. "I couldn't get his attention. He's been looking at his feet for ages."

Ronald blanched. He could see Arkle limbering up and her muscles stretching the pattern in her tweeds like an ordnance survey map of the hills.

He ran.

Arkle straightened up and caught sight of Ronald leaping over a dry-stone wall three fields away. She let out a bellow and set off in pursuit.

Margery and Henry exchanged a kiss and linked arms. "That'll be a draw, then," she said.

The wind sighed, the thatch rippled and little groups of Valley folk holding steaming cups of forever debatable liquid watched as the sponsors tried to salvage something twisted from the distant pond.

The only sound to remotely spoil the mood was the steady flap-flap sound and the jingling of a broken golden chain as the Black Swan came in from the East.

THE END

144

About the Author

Patrick Barrett is a sixty year old ex-miner from Mansfield in Nottinghamshire. He is married to Paula and between them, they have several children. 'Shakespeare's Cuthbert' was his first book, though he has been writing comedy for several years.

His aims as a writer are 'to be successful and make people laugh by providing them with an escape from the harshness of real life'.

His other abiding interest is in antiques.